THROUGH SHADOWS SLOW

ABRAHAM BOYARSKY

8TH HOUSE PUBLISHING

8th House Publishing
Montreal, Canada

Copyright © 8th House Publishing 2019
First Edition

ISBN 978-1-926716-57-2

Published worldwide by 8th House Publishing.
Front Cover Design by 8th House Publishing

Designed by 8th House Publishing.
www.8thHousePublishing.com

Set in Garamond, Delicious Heavy, Raleway and Caslon.

Library and Archives Canada Cataloguing in Publication

Title: Through shadows slow / Abraham Boyarsky.
Names: Boyarsky, Abraham, author.
Identifiers: Canadiana 20190170808 | ISBN 9781926716572 (softcover)
Classification: LCC PS8553.O932 T47 2019 | DDC C813/.54—dc23

THROUGH SHADOWS SLOW
Abraham Boyarsky

Dedicated to Edward Carson

Contents

I- Jerusalem 5

II- The North...........................36

III - Masada...........................164

I

❧

JERUSALEM

❧

March 17, 2014

THE THREE-HOUR DELAY at the Zürich airport didn't diminish the old doctor's hope that he'd make it to the cemetery before nightfall. Toting a small luggage bag, he charged out of the Tel Aviv terminal into the bright evening sunlight. Although Daniel Edelman was in his eighties, he was as tall and straight as in his youth, with a full head of cotton white hair. Holding up one arm to hail a taxi, he stepped directly into the fierce traffic. His son, a heavyset man in his fifties, on his way to an ophthalmology conference in Jerusalem, lunged forward to grab his father's arm and drew him back to the safety of the sidewalk.

"Please don't be nervous," he implored, holding his father's arm tightly with both hands. "The cemetery is a short drive from the hotel. God willing, we'll get up early in the morning and go together."

"I'm not nervous!" Daniel snapped, shaking himself free. His son's platitudes, forever laced with religious undertones, annoyed him. Besides, he did not like the idea of Benjamin accompanying him to the cemetery. He needed to go alone this time. Thirteen years had passed since they last visited Daniel's wife, whose mysterious will had brought her body to the Holy Land more than thirty years ago.

A taxi pulled up to the curb. Father and son got into the back seat of a late model German car.

"Clarion Hotel Jerusalem," Daniel said, panting from the heat. Beads of sweat glistened on his forehead.

"I know it's in Jerusalem!" the driver snapped. "You pay U.S. dollars?"

"Yes," Benjamin answered.

"One hundred dollars."

Benjamin struggled to extract the wallet from his back pants pocket, then paid the driver.

Long shadows of palm trees swerved left then right as the cab raced out of the airport. Daniel stared through the closed window at the verdant landscape. Soon they were in the countryside. Daniel gazed upon the rainbows formed by the sprinklers watering the vegetable fields. Benjamin took no notice of the fields or the iridescent arches shimmering with wet light. His eyes were lowered to a Judaic text spread open across his lap. A black skull cap listed precariously on his bald pate. His prominent cheekbones and a gap between his upper front teeth were undeniable inheritances from his mother. It troubled the old cardiologist that he was never able to see himself in his son's features.

"This is our third trip?" Daniel asked uneasily, the tremor in his right hand more pronounced than usual.

"Fourth," his son corrected him. "1980, 1990, 2001, and now."

"I wasn't counting the first time when we buried her."

"I understand," Benjamin said softly, then reverted to the holy book now inclined toward the window to catch the waning sunlight.

"Don't you have to prepare for your lecture?" Daniel asked, his voice modulated by a nuance of displeasure intended to remind Benjamin that he was wasting time with his religious studies.

"It's done."

This was how Benjamin informed his father that he had already prepared the lecture, avoiding any trace of personal credit. They drove on for another ten minutes. Benjamin turned to look at his father. The old man's head was leaning against the window, his eyes closed. Daniel had shaved the day before leaving Montreal, but now his cheeks were covered with a white fuzz, concealing some of the deep wrinkles.

Benjamin had sensed the unnatural reserve between his parents from an early age. His earliest memories of his father were of a successful doctor, an intellectual, but a man who was unsociable and sorrowful, a man who helped many people but did not love humanity. His mother was a kind, self-educated woman whose *joie de vivre* had been eroded by her husband's relentless indifference. Benjamin was able to trace his father's gradual descent into depression after his mother's passing.

Until his retirement a few years ago, Daniel's cardiology practice had kept him on an even keel. But for someone who had never rested a moment, to whom idleness was abhorrent, retirement provided too much time to ponder the past. Painful memories snapped at his sanity, breaching the ramparts he had carefully constructed around his life-story.

Sensing his son's eyes on him, Daniel opened his and asked: "Do you remember your mother?"

"Yes. I was twenty when she passed away."

"Thirty-four years ago?"

"Yes."

Stroking his beard, Benjamin continued contemplating his father, unable to penetrate his sadness. His thoughts turned to his teenage years when he was caught between seminary teachers who saw in him a brilliant Talmudic scholar and his father who demanded a practical career such as medicine. Benjamin tried to follow both paths, and by the age of eighteen had bleeding ulcers. Finally, with the permission of the rabbis, he entered medical school in New York, pursuing his religious studies secretly in the late hours of the night.

After decades of virtual solitude, Daniel now responded to minor situations with excessive emotion, often gesticulating impatiently to emphasize arguments his words failed to convey. Benjamin was very different in nature. When stopped by people in his community with medical issues, he was patient and polite, maintaining a pose of deep contemplation as he listened. With rabbinic precision, he considered the information before uttering a few precise words of advice. When rain threatened, he left home with an umbrella and when doffing his glasses, it was always with both hands on the arms—things the older, nervous Edelman would never do.

Content with his lot, Benjamin conducted his life on the secure foundation of family and community. His two older daughters were married to religious scholars. One lived in Brooklyn, the other in Lakewood, New Jersey. Three younger children were still at home, all gifted and happy, attending Jewish schools. One of them expressed an interest in studying medicine, following in the footsteps of his father and grandfather. The grandchildren respected the elderly doctor but, being unobservant, he felt alienated from them. The previous winter when Daniel had pneumonia, Benjamin insisted that he stay with his family. Daniel tried for a few days, but then stealthily left the house with all its religious restrictions and returned to his apartment where he waited to die.

⟫⟪

AN ACCIDENT on the highway had halted the flow of traffic. On the opposite side of the median, a car was on fire and ambulances and fire trucks were clogging both sides of the highway. Meanwhile the taxi driver turned off the air conditioning and it was getting unbearably hot inside the cab. The old man got out, followed by his son. Benjamin was about six inches shorter than his father, broad shouldered and rotund. From the high vantage point on the highway, they saw the sun dissolving into a band of orange along the Mediterranean. The smell of freshly cut grass wafted from nearby fields, a redolence that reminded Daniel of his childhood days in Poland before the war.

"Do you remember Evelyn Ramer?" Daniel asked.

"Mommy often talked about her. She lived in Sainte-Agathe in the fifties."

"Her daughter, Sandra, moved to Jerusalem twenty years ago. Sandra sent me an email last month asking when I would visit. There are things that belonged to your mother she wants to give me."

"Is that why you decided to come?" Benjamin queried.

The old man shrugged his shoulders. He did not know the answer. Stepping between stopped cars, he made his way to the median for a better look at the smouldering vehicle in the distance, glanced anxiously at his watch, and finally had to admit there was no chance of arriving at the cemetery before nightfall.

At last the traffic began moving. Father and son re-entered the cab. Daniel seated himself next to the driver. At the outskirts of Jerusalem, traffic slowed to a crawl. When the driver gave up an opportunity to pass a car ahead of him, Daniel lost patience. He turned to the driver and said brazenly: "If you don't want to drive, let me take over!" He even made a move to grab the wheel.

Benjamin leaned forward and implored: "Father, please."

"He can go much faster," Daniel protested, having forgotten that a few minutes earlier he had abandoned hope of reaching the cemetery before nightfall.

Intermittent streams of headlights outlined the traffic ahead of them. In the twilight distance, a veil of desert dust hung over Jerusalem. When they finally arrived, the city streets were congested with automobiles and pedestrian traffic. Passing through a cacophony of honking and shouting, the cab finally stopped in front of the Clarion Hotel. A light drizzle from a nearby garden hose dappled the white flagstone sidewalk as father and son entered the hotel.

⸻

DANIEL stepped onto the small veranda on the sixth floor of the hotel while Benjamin unpacked. He grasped the balustrade to stop the tremors in his right hand. In the rush to accompany his son, Daniel had forgotten to pack his medications. He had realized it on the plane but didn't mention it to Benjamin. Squinting, he peered into the darkness beyond the illuminated walls of the Old City towards the Mount of Olives.

⸻

DANIEL was unable to sleep. After Benjamin had fallen into the quiet, regular breathing of deep sleep, Daniel made his way down to the lobby where a group of mathematicians had just arrived for a conference at the Hebrew University. The doctor was wearing a short sleeve shirt. A tall, blond mathematician from Australia, identified by a tag on his chest, noticed the numbers on Daniel's forearm. He thought for a moment as the old man shuffled past him, then pointing to the doctor's forearm, he said: "That's a prime number you have there, sir."

Daniel glanced at the number 104723 that had been tattooed on his forearm at the age of twelve. He never imagined there was anything special about his number. Uncomfortable in places where strangers greeted each other with smiles, Daniel stepped out to the terrace behind the lobby. A one-eyed black cat emerged from a labyrinth of lanes and slunk toward him in the darkness. Daniel hissed loudly to chase it away, but the cat did not budge. At its own good pace it slithered into a shadow. Motes danced in beams of light aimed up along the white stone wall to the top of the building where Israeli flags lolled in the sultry night air. Strands of spider webs glimmered, strummed by the warm desert breeze.

The old doctor walked through narrow side streets as shadows of bats criss-crossed the cobblestones beneath his feet. All at once he heard human sounds. Approaching the source Daniel found himself mounting the broken steps of an ancient synagogue. He paused to look up at the narrow front balconies that notched the upper floors where young men stood praying. Daniel observed them for a while, then moved on, wondering how his life would have turned out had he followed friends to Palestine after the war. Instead a whim had brought him to Canada where he got married, graduated from medical school, and led an uneventful life practicing cardiology. Then his wife was diagnosed with terminal breast cancer.

Daniel ordered a glass of orange juice at a kiosk, plodded back to the hotel, and took the elevator to his room. He fell asleep and dreamt of the north: a woman was sitting on a horse smiling down at him; then he was in a forest with his father, struggling to keep him on his feet. Awakening in a sweat, Daniel glanced at the window and was relieved to see that the day had dawned. Barefoot, he stepped past his sleeping son whose legs poked out from under the blanket. Daniel remarked again how the side view of Benjamin's head sharpened his resemblance to his mother. He drew the blanket over his son's feet.

Daniel glanced into the bathroom mirror and winced. Every few years he grudgingly accepted a deteriorated image mirrors foisted on him. He reached for a cup and filled it with water to rinse his mouth. It fell out of his trembling hand onto his darkly veined feet. When he came out of the bathroom, Daniel found Benjamin standing near the window draped in a prayer shawl.

"I'm going down for a coffee," Daniel said.

But he had other plans.

꧁꧂

THERE WAS a large photo of Masada in the lobby advertising a daily half-day tour leaving the hotel at 1:15. The idea of climbing the mountain appealed to Daniel, if only he had the strength. Feeling groggy from lack of sleep, he bent down to a water dispenser, drank a few mouthfuls and stepped outside, squinting into the bright sunlight. There was still an hour until the cemetery gates would open. He planned to walk for awhile, then take a taxi. As the sun ascended from the direction of Bethlehem, cats slunk out of alleys to bask in pools of light. Children scurried through the streets in little swarms, and gaunt, middle-aged men, clipping black portfolios, marched briskly into modern buildings with glass curtain facades. Suddenly, a hand reached out from the flow of pedestrians and pulled Daniel aside. A smiling, orthodox young man with long side locks offered a skull cap with one hand and phylacteries with the other. Daniel ignored him and walked away. Further on, a bent man in black garb shook a charity box— the pauper's tambourine—in front of Daniel's face. He dropped a coin into the can and continued toward a row of taxis parked beyond cement bollards that protected against vehicular attacks. Entering a taxi, Daniel asked to be taken to the Mount of Olives Cemetery. The cab drove through the awakening streets of the city, past food vendors opening their kiosks and beggars squatting on street corners. Descending into Kidron Valley, the cab continued along winding streets bordered by high stone walls. Across the valley, the Old City was bathed in morning sunlight. There was a commotion at a police observation post. Palestinian youths had thrown rocks at a tour bus. A window was shattered and a young American woman had been injured. Police officers were trying to restore calm.

The taxi stopped at a high metal gate. Daniel stepped through and was greeted by the sight of thousands of flat white stone monuments on a wide mountain slope. Daniel sidled past the graves of prophets and politicians, recognizing landmarks from earlier visits. His heart was beating quickly as he approached his wife's grave. Many of the monuments were sprinkled with stones. Gilla's was bare. He assumed that no one had been here for more than a decade. Turning his back to the blazing sun, he began to speak: "I'm sorry for not coming earlier. There were opportunities, but for each one there was an excuse: pneumonia last winter, a UTI the year before, and high blood pressure the year before that. The delights of old age. Benjamin is attending a conference at the university here, so I tagged along. It's a long trip. How I wish you had chosen a resting place closer to home. But this was your will, which I never understood but respected. This is such a dry land; wherever one turns, there is only rock and sand. If a scrap of grass sprouts up audaciously, here or there, it's so conspicuous it hurts the eyes. The sun contorts my face and makes me look mean. It bleaches away memory. This morning I took a short walk and within a few minutes I was gasping for air, drenched in sweat. But I'm here because here our essences meet; here there is nothing to hide. I'm sure you miss the forests and the lakes of the north as I do. How you loved the foaming summer foliage, the lakes and rivers at every turn. And so I will begin my story in the forests around Sainte-Agathe with the stuttering of old and painful memories. I loved the forests and the ubiquitous shadows where I hid from the sun. When I first arrived in the north I felt that I didn't deserve to live, but you saw in me something which I never would have found. For that I am forever grateful to you. Although I don't remember what I did a few days ago, the memories of the distant past are agonizingly vivid. They gain clarity as I grow older, revealing details I had forgotten for many years. I cling to these memories, bound to you by them, but my own presence in them is elusive. I am there and I am not there, both dead and alive like Schrödinger's cat. I see little islands strewn across the undulating surface of time. I tip toe from one island to the other as I slide ineluctably into the black hole of memory. There, on the event horizon beyond which there is no escape, I see the *shtetl* of my childhood when Jews lived in the numbing stupor of religion that silenced all premonition of danger. I touch my mother through the gossamer web of space-time. It is raining and I see myself walking with her along puddled streets, past synagogues and bustling markets. Mother says, 'May the rain wash away all our sins.' 'What are sins?' I ask. 'Sins are bad things people do to other people.' 'People don't do bad things,' is my riposte. I see my father who was born at the turn of the twentieth century, and my grandfather who was born in the 1870s. And here I stand alone in the twenty-first century, a crumbling old bridge straddling a century. I see myself in childhood and now in old age, two thin slices of bread, an empty sandwich of time. I careen through the years, brief happy years before the war. After the war, I cringe within silence. I say to myself: 'I will write the story of my life with six words.' And so I reduce my possessions to the size of a thumbnail and fling it to the wind. The wind takes me across the ocean and I am with you that first summer in the north when we manacled time with dreams. I see you indistinctly through the morning mist on the shores of the lake where we first made eye contact. Your voice calls to me from my subconscious: 'Daniel, Daniel the lions are gone. You can now leave the den you built around you.' Gilla, you're a pointillist image against the lake behind you. I smear the dots together and construe the misery on your face I had inflicted on you later that summer. There is a parting at the train station as I head off to medical school. You bring me gloves and a bag of fruit. I should have a clear image of you, but I have to reconstruct you from details: long red hair, wisps dangling over your freckled brow, your right nipple scarred over from the fire on your sixth birthday, the remains of the dress you wore at that party and which I once saw in the attic of your parents' home. And so I summon you from the hodgepodge of memories, an attractive young woman of medium height with slightly disproportionately short legs. 'Gilla' means joy in Hebrew, a name that captured the very essence of who you were before I destroyed you. As I descended the hill to your grave just now, I felt the heaviness of the Canadian winter in my legs, a thick black vector of lead pointed straight down to the center of the earth. I see ice whorls, their fractal arms swirling away from the window of my room in the TB hospital up north. I hate the heat, but I must confess I can no longer tolerate the cold either. I trudge like a penguin through the snow-covered streets in my heavy boots, my torso bent precariously forward. In a Canadian winter you feel like you're inside a container, large at first, so you're not aware of the walls. But as the winter progresses the walls contract. You feel increasingly small and immobile until you're hopelessly trapped in a white box called winter. And although I've experienced it more than sixty times, I've never gotten over the claustrophobia of the snow walls along icy streets, the ponderous clouds overhead. Those were the winters of our youth when I ran through blizzards to bring you grapes wrapped in silk the colour of your eyes. But now I feel every chill in my bones. I recall a Sunday when we were standing at the corner of Cedar and Dr. Penfield. You're wearing a blue jacket, unbuttoned, hood off as usual. Behind you blue fingers of ice cover the rocky outcroppings. Your head is tilted, smiling, a puff of snow powder veiling your face. I take a photo with your camera. The long months of winter have been playing cat and mouse with my moods. Friends tell me to spend winter in Florida. Benjamin, too, is pushing me. But what would I do there? Solve crossword puzzles on the beach? As enticement, an old friend fixed me up with a Russian woman who spends her winters in Miami. I did not tell you this the last time I was here, but twenty years ago I went on a date with her. As soon as I sniffed the pungent perfume and glimpsed at her darkly freckled chest, I turned away in disgust. You were clean. Your scar never bothered me because I knew from the first time I saw it that I was your scar. This past winter I slipped on the ice and bruised my hip. My luck is running out. Time is the worst predator. I go to dance classes twice a week. Dance with Parkinson's they call it. Can you imagine anything more absurd? I was diagnosed with the disease two years ago. When we waded into middle age together, I was comforted by the thought that in old age we would accompany each other to medical specialists and sit side by side, holding hands in the crowded waiting rooms. Now there is no one to fret for my health. I go alone and observe the Asian patients from whom I cannot expect any succour. They don't know what a Jew is and have never heard of the Holocaust. But I'm hanging in, as they say. I try to redefine myself in these circumstances and I have an absurd thought: I'm an orphan who has not seen his mother in seventy-three years, his father in seventy years, an old crane, spreading its ragged wings, waiting for one last upward breeze. On looking back, I realize that the things I feared most were never a danger to me at all. I imagine a place where one does not feel the cold or the heat, where one is never hungry or thirsty, and where one's clothing does not wear out. This place exists and even has a name; it's called Death. But nothing to be afraid of. It's only an angstrom, a nanosecond beyond life, so close I can touch it. And so I'm as close to you now as that night when I saw you and your mother clandestinely leaving the Mount Sinai Hospital after your abortion… I look back again to our first summer when I had hoped we would meld our disparities into a meaningful life together. I see us during our most intimate moment: You're beneath me, but at the instant of consummation my dead father appears at your side and I collapse on top of him to keep him from freezing to death on our final march. You and he are inextricably interwoven in my memories. How patiently you waited while my father's memory foiled all attempts at intimacy. I see us canoeing in and out of the amorphous mists of our history. I believed there was a time when you understood me and what I had lived through, soothing the contusions and the bitter silence that defined me. But you had been exposed to too many things at a young age, poisoning you for life with one man. You were good to me but you were also good to many others, leaving me with an ache in my heart which never left. Nonetheless there was an innocence about you, an unadorned simplicity, a raw, disarming purity, and so I tried to join you in the life of the forest. I remember when you laughed at almost anything and we both know what your fickle bladder did whenever you laughed too hard. Gilla, do you remember the time when we kissed on a street corner in Sainte-Agathe under a white lilac tree? 'What do you think, this is Paris?' you chuckled, then burst into laughter so uncontrollable that I feared you would flood the street. Now that I live more and more in the past, morsels of memories are the scanty meals that sustain me. I recall a man who lost his life on the ship coming over from the German DP camps. The wind blew his hat off. He had reached for it instinctively, leaning over the railing on the deck, went too far, and plummeted into the Atlantic. All for a hat. Perhaps the war had taught him the value of a hat. And is it any different with me? Looking back, I see the life I had lost over a glimpse from the beach. I could have forgotten it as one forgets a hat lost in the ocean. Instead I reached for it beyond the railing of memory and fell into an abyss of bitterness. My memories of you are from so long ago, that I clump them together with those of my childhood in the *shtetl*. I long for you as I long for my parents and my saintly grandfather who had tried to mould me into a Torah scholar. I see you as a little girl in your birthday dress before the fire. Then I see us in the fields behind the Jewish hotels. There, in the high grass, we finally consummated our love even as my joy was sullied by the promise I made to my dying father to never be happy. Now we are at my graduation from medical school. The lower campus of McGill University is crowded with students and their relatives. I stand between you and your mother for a photograph at the Roddick Gates. Your father had died the year before. You're wearing high heels and a short blue skirt, all smiles, your long red hair on your shoulders, glistening in the sunlight. Dr. Marquis, Mrs. Ramer, Anita, Hershel and their eight year old twins are present. For a moment I feel I have a family…

"On the plane here, I was thinking how strange it is that man has to pass through a woman's body to reach the Garden of Eden. This is how God tricks mankind into reproducing. And so you gave birth to Benjamin. I was with you in the delivery room. I saw it all. How I worried over every detail of the boy's life, never explaining to him the demons that controlled my actions. I would virtually force-feed Benjamin, as if by feeding him I was feeding the starving children I had seen succumb in the camps. By any logic Benjamin should have grown into a neurotic adult, not the unruffled eye surgeon and happily married family man he has become. He is definitely your son. As Benjamin grew older, his features confirmed my worst fear—that I was not in his genes. I see Benjamin, a toddler with a red hat and large white bon-bon on top, as I trundle him through the autumn streets of Sainte-Agathe. He points to the sky with its myriad of little disjoint white clouds and cries out perceptively: 'Puzzle! Puzzle!' The special bond between you and him was never more apparent to me than on a day in October when Benjamin was four years old. You're sitting on a bench while Benjamin climbs to the top of a slide in the playground on Fletcher's Field. You throw an imaginary rope to him which he catches laughingly. Then you slowly pull the rope toward you, one hand after the other, while Benjamin holds the other end with both hands, allowing himself to be drawn down the slide by the invisible rope between mother and son. I watch enviously from a distance. I wanted to be that rope, to join your friendship. I know you would have allowed me in, but I was afraid to love.

"I wonder if you remember the day I took Benjamin to a synagogue on St. Urbain Street. He was six years old. It was the anniversary of my father's death during the final march, the one time a year I entered a synagogue. While Benjamin and I waited for the evening service, a young man with a red beard sat down next to Benjamin and opened a prayer book to the first page displaying the letters of the Hebrew alphabet. He pointed to the first letter, the aleph, and encouraged Benjamin to read it, but he did not know how. The man was surprised and asked me which school Benjamin attended. I refused to answer. I did not want to communicate with these men.

A few days later I discovered that this man visited our house when I was not home and convinced you that the boy should attend the Hebrew school nearby. I did not have the strength to intervene and so Benjamin was enrolled. Then one day Benjamin dropped the prayer book he had brought home from school. He picked it up quickly from the floor and kissed the cover. I looked on with surprise, suddenly aware that I had lost my son. As time went on, you and I saw in the growing boy what we failed to find in our marriage. I cannot say that I had no influence on him: as a boy of seven or eight he was determined to tattoo his forearm with the same numbers I have on my arm.

"I taught Benjamin his first lesson in science at the Fletcher's Field playground. I lifted him onto a seesaw. While his end was down, I went to the other end. By pushing down and pulling up, I raised and lowered the boy. Then as I sat down on my end, Benjamin lunged upward, where he remained joyfully perched. The seesaw would not move even as the boy bounced up and down. Smiling, I moved closer to the center. As I inched toward the center, the seesaw attained a wondrous equilibrium, oscillating ever so slightly in an endless, self-sustaining motion.

"The religious school you sent him to molded him into a little fanatic. In his childhood diary which you encouraged him to keep, he wrote: 'Leible started it, but I said, I'm sorry because I want the Messiah to come.' I've been rambling... Now I will explain the reason I have come. If only I knew where to start. I see you as a middle age woman, a dignified lady, but slightly pathetic in your attempt to look young. You've dyed your hair blond, parted down the middle where the roots are inexorably white. The dimples in your cheeks are more pronounced than in your youth. Under a precisely tousled bang, you're wearing enormous black sunglasses to conceal your wrinkles. I once saw you coming out of an elevator wearing those sunglasses. Recently, I saw a woman in an elevator with a tiny growth on the tip of her nose, hardly noticeable, but to me it was a Pinocchio nose *in potentia*. You see, I've become hopelessly cynical in old age. The good news though is that, at last, I've retired from my practice. You may recall those early years when my clientele consisted only of survivors. I listened to their stories and, pretending to be a cardiologist of the soul, I tried to heal their broken hearts. Inevitably the Yiddish language vanished from my office on Esplanade Street across Fletcher's Field. The Jews moved into affluent areas of the city and found new doctors in medical buildings. New patients began appearing, Asian immigrants and young French Canadians who had invaded the plateau. They came with drug addictions and venereal diseases, and I no longer enjoyed my practice. To them the Nazi crimes were as venial as a baby's tantrum. I look back at my career which amounted to a few mediocre research papers on heart function. I was always silent on evolution at conferences, and that silence, the silence of a Holocaust survivor, spoke volumes to my scientific colleagues. With silence I defended God in the corridors of academia. Not that I chose to out of fear. I had nothing to fear. Dear Gilla, there I go again off on a tangent, and I haven't yet touched on the real reason for which I've come. I never had time to unravel the source of my incorrigible sadness while I was occupied for long hours with my practice. It burdened our marriage and brought you here prematurely. I mentioned elevators a moment ago. Curious, because I didn't intend to. I don't know why it sprang to mind, but whenever I'm in an elevator, I recall a casual comment you once made, that if you had met me for the first time in an elevator and I had propositioned you, you would have immediately accepted. You thought you were complimenting me, but this seemingly innocent remark tormented me for sixty years. Was it a compliment about me or rather a statement about a dissolute past? Would you have accepted almost anyone who propositioned you? After all, what was special about me, a phobic survivor who had barely survived? I hope you're beginning to understand the drift of my words. Yes, I have always been convinced of your promiscuity. I became an expert at exaggerating and deciphering your lustful thoughts in my jealous mind. Your notarized will was the last proverbial straw. I imagined scenarios that would have led to your strange decision to be buried in Jerusalem. No doubt that red-haired Israeli dancer had made promises or whispered into your ear that he was born in Jerusalem and planned to spend his life there. Your unrequited love for him would have accounted for the will. You were uneducated and assimilated in your youth, immersed in the French-Canadian culture of beer and square dancing. Why would you insist on being buried in Jerusalem? That night in August of '52, in the forest, he must have said something to you that burgeoned in your heart throughout the years until you decided that if you could not be near your lover in life, then you would be near him in death. And so now I have relieved myself of the worst. It may very well be that all I have said is based on nothing more than circumstance, but how often does one have direct, hard proof of anything? My chest is clear, having finally said what I have kept concealed. Now I want to tell you that I have forgiven you and I hope that you might forgive me for having neither released you nor loved you, but rather having forced you to live with me in the limbo between. This is how I punished you and myself. I never said a word to you, but the pain of seeing you walk away from the beach with that dancer festered in my heart for sixty years, tainting even the happiest of moments together. This cataclysmic event, together with your abortion in the TB hospital which we never talked about, and your elevator comment, became part of a pattern which later, with Benjamin's birth and the will that brought you here, formed a straight line from which the condemning extrapolation was blatantly evident. In my thoughts you were a lady of grandiose gestures, kissing me, a TB patient in the mouth, but promiscuous between the gestures. How was I to measure the spikes of joy against the odious facts between them? This was the dilemma of my early years with you. To admit that I was jealous would have meant I was a normal man. Had I not seen what I witnessed in the camps, I might have forgiven you early on or, at least interpreted things in a more positive light. In fact, now and again, there were moments when I felt a tinge of doubt. I thought, perhaps there are reasonable explanations for what I saw that night on the beach and for all my other suspicions. But my war experiences had distorted the evidence beyond plausible explanation. I remember a patient who had been an NKVD officer for Stalin. Even long after he had settled in Canada, he could not stop interrogating everyone he met. I asked myself again and again, 'What right do I have to complain?' I who had repeatedly eluded the gas chambers. I should have been content, indeed happy, with every modicum of affection from you, even if I had to share you with others. How utterly ungrateful I had been! I should have pursued such thoughts, but fearing confirmation of my worst fears, I always created a gap between suspicion and fact, and in that cleft of uncertainty, I subsisted on a diet of minimal love. A bubble pops up from the mud, then sinks slowly back into the quagmire of time. Gilla, one last word. No matter whatever else, I envied your zest for life. The genes for this characteristic had been excised from my DNA in the camps."

Daniel suddenly became aware of Benjamin standing behind him. He did not know how long he had been there reciting prayers from a little book, tears flowing down his cheeks. A sustained glance between father and son exposed a distraught look in the old man's eyes as each one tried to gauge the other's understanding of the dead woman's life.

Daniel nodded solemnly, bent down to pick up a stone, then placed it on top of the monument. He read the inscription one more time and stepped back with a heavy heart. As his father passed by, Benjamin turned to the grave, whispered a few words, then followed his father out of the cemetery.

Daniel had hoped for a cathartic experience that could have relieved him of the burden of memory, but he was leaving as troubled as ever. Nothing had changed. The pressure in his chest had not subsided.

Benjamin told his father on the way back to the hotel that his plenary talk had gone well. There was only one more session he had to attend in the afternoon and he reminded him that their return flight was scheduled to leave at five the next morning. Daniel nodded but did not care to know the details of the return trip. His late morning meeting with Sandra was planned at a café near the hotel. He would return to the hotel afterwards and go on the half-day ascent of Masada. Daniel knew Benjamin wouldn't like the idea so he didn't mention it.

⊰⊱

DANIEL sat down at a round white table in the midday sunlight at Café 77 on Yafo Street. Israeli music played in the background. Black posts punctuated the edges of the sidewalk, to which motorcycles were secured. Mothers trundling carriages jostled with armed soldiers on the bustling streets amid the noise of traffic.

A waitress approached with a menu. Daniel ordered coffee and toast. His mouth was dry and he felt dizzy. This was his second day without his medication.

He remembered Sandra as a tall thin girl who had carried letters to him from Gilla—letters he had refused to read. When an elderly woman holding a cane and carrying an old leather briefcase emerged from the flow of pedestrians, he saw that old age had shrunk her neck and bent her back. Daniel recognized Sandra's mother in her face. Standing up to greet her, they embraced for a moment, then sat down.

"It's so good to see you," she said, smiling. He observed her blemished and withered arms. "I had a stroke four years ago."

"Sorry to hear that," he replied caringly.

"I'm much better now. I'm walking again."

Daniel told her he had just come from visiting his wife on the Mount of Olives. Sandra said that she had gone a few times in recent years. Although Sandra was a few years younger, she and Gilla had been best friends.

Sandra queried: "How is Benjy? I remember him growing up. He and Gilla were inseparable. But you... you were afraid to love him."

Daniel was taken aback by her blunt observation.

"I did my best," he muttered, blushing.

He took out a black and white photo from his shirt pocket and handed it to her. Sandra and her mother were standing with Gilla at the public beach in Sainte-Agathe, all three wearing full black bathing suits. Sandra smiled, then turned the photo over and read the date: July 26, 1952. She extended it to Daniel, but he refused to take it back. "Please keep it. It's difficult for me to look at." Then he diverted the conversation: "Why did you decide to live in Jerusalem?"

"I was alone in Montreal after my husband died. My daughters were married and had moved to Israel years earlier. I followed them here. It's as simple as that. I suppose you knew that I had a crush on you. Even when you were in the hospital you were tall and handsome. Gilla never stopped talking about you. When you broke up that fall she nearly died. Do you remember her letters I delivered to you before you left to study in Montreal? You were so angry you refused to open them."

Daniel lowered his eyes.

The waitress handed Sandra a menu. She did not need it and ordered a glass of ice water. "I'm on a strict diet," she said. "My sugar levels are all over the place."

She looked thoughtfully at Daniel then placed her hand on the briefcase. "Before Gilla died… She gave my mother her briefcase," Sandra said. "I found it in her house after she passed away. When I moved to Jerusalem I brought it with me. I never opened it… I want you to have it."

A taxi arrived for Sandra. She and Daniel resolved to meet again, although both knew it would most likely never happen. Alone at the table, Daniel sat back down and opened the briefcase. He drew out a yellow hard covered notebook, frayed at the corners.

He turned to the first page and read:

My name is Gilla. I am 11 years old. My mother told me that today is December 9, 1942. I just want to write that a French boy tried to kiss me after school so I kicked him in the foot.

On another page she wrote:

My father talks about a war where Jews are getting killed. I have a friend Stella is her name. The teacher hit a boy on the hand with a ruler. Now he is a good boy. The best. Good-bye dear diary, I love you.

He skimmed through the entries of her adolescent years, brief descriptions of friendships with boys and girls. The traffic in front of Daniel had come to a complete standstill. Drivers left their vehicles and were shouting at each other. In the midst of the chaos, it suddenly occurred to Daniel that Gilla might have made an entry about that fateful night in August of '52 when she had left the beach with the Israeli dancer. He turned the pages, but was afraid to see.

II

⚘

THE NORTH

⚘

Late October, 1951.

THE TRAIN SWAGGERED through the industrial neighborhoods of the city and then gaining speed, headed north into the gray, autumn countryside. A shabbily dressed young man sat alone, coughing blood into a towel. He leaned his head against the cold window, gazing at the tawny fields flitting by. The flat landscape became snow-powdered forested hills, calling to mind terrain of Eastern Poland. He could almost see the SS officer lying in the snow, arms serenely crossed on his chest, his frozen genitals stuck in his mouth—a notice from Russian partisans. Daniel Edelman's thoughts swirled through the war years, DP camps in Germany, a crowded immigrant ship, and now a train which was bringing him to a hospital in the Laurentian Mountains north of Montreal.

The train came to a stop at the village of Sainte-Agathe. Daniel collected his valise, a bag of English books, and a rolled-up x-ray film. Wearing the long black coat and ankle-high running shoes the Jewish Immigration Service in Montreal had given him, he stepped onto the wooden platform. He stood in the bracing wind, the frigid air gurgling painfully in his ailing lungs. A middle-aged woman wearing a brown fur coat identified the tall, gaunt young man from among the arrivals. She introduced herself in faltering Yiddish: "My name is Evelyn Ramer. I've come to take you to the hospital."

A cab was waiting for them at the front entrance. Daniel followed her through the station. She was a large woman with a waddling gait. Once they were seated in the back, Evelyn said: "Just last week I brought another patient to the Mount Sinai Hospital."

The driver lit a cigarette, then glanced in the mirror at the emaciated figure in the back seat. Daniel rolled down the window and coughed stridently.

"Pierre, please stop smoking! You know it's not healthy for our patient!" Evelyn reprimanded the driver, who immediately spat the cigarette into the snow. "My Yiddish is pathetic. Do you understand English?" she asked, meeting Daniel's eyes.

"I understand," he replied. He had learned English from American soldiers in Germany with whom he had traded smuggled cigarettes for chocolates.

Touching the hem of Daniel's coat, she remarked: "You can't wear this skimpy thing up here!"

They drove past a large church with a wide snow-covered stairway protruding into the street, reminding

Daniel of his grandfather's imposing white beard, spread open like an apron over his chest. A lake was visible between buildings to the right and through the small oval back window. Daniel glimpsed at the quiet village receding into the deepening dusk.

Evelyn was a cheerful, garrulous woman with a smooth, unblemished complexion and a becoming smile. She began relating the story she told every new arrival, of the origins of the hospital and the town. "Many people in Montreal were dying of tuberculosis at the turn of the century," she began. "After it was discovered that the fresh air of the Laurentian Mountains could cure TB, the Mount Sinai Hospital was built in 1909. Family members wanted to be close to their sick relatives, so boarding houses and hotels sprang up in Sainte-Agathe. Twelve years ago my husband came here for the cure." She sighed at the memory of her husband. "Rest, healthy food, and fresh air—that was the only treatment then. It was before the war. At first I visited him every week, but the trip from the city was long, especially in the winter, and I couldn't leave the children. The third year I bought a house on the lake to be close to Nathan. I stayed on after he passed away. My son lives in Montreal, and Sandra my sixteen year-old daughter, is here with me. The volunteer work for the hospital keeps me busy all day. It wouldn't get done if I wasn't here."

They crossed a narrow wooden bridge. The somber expression on Daniel's face made Evelyn imagine he was concerned about social life in the north. "Don't worry about activities up here. There's no synagogue yet, but we have an active sisterhood. In the summer, Jews from New York come for vacation. I can't understand a word of their Galician Yiddish. The men play cards night and day. Last year Anita and her husband Hershel moved up here from Montreal to run an afternoon Yiddish program for the children. They were in the concentration camps like you." On uttering these words, Evelyn covered her mouth with both hands, eyes agape. She had been warned many times not to mention the camps to survivors. Fortunately, there was no sign of emotion on Daniel's face. Relieved, she went on: "I'm sure you've heard of the famous Anita Kreisman. She was an actress in Warsaw before the war. Her parents were born in Russia. Her father was a Trotskyite. Stalin murdered him in the summer of '34. A month later, her mother took her own life in a Moscow subway station. An aunt in Warsaw took Anita in. What an asset she has been to our little community! She's even planning a Hanukah play with the children."

Daniel listened but had nothing to say.

"I can't wait for you to meet my son," Evelyn went on. "He's in law school. In the winter he comes up to ski. Sometimes he even visits his mother," she quipped with a rippling little laugh that reconfigured her face for the worse.

Moments later, a large white building loomed out of the darkling forest.

"We're here," Evelyn announced as the taxi made its way up the steep, curving road under a canopy of naked tree crowns and past a frozen pond on their left.

"This way," Evelyn beckoned. Daniel followed her up the stone steps to a white portico. They walked through one of the arched openings into the main lobby of the hospital. A Star of David was engraved into a large maple plaque on the main wall. Daniel looked around, inhaled the scent of ammonia, and fainted.

⊷⊱⊰⊷

SHADOWS whispering in French slithered across the walls of Daniel's room during the night. He dreamt of his mother. He's an infant in her arms, her forearm against the child's damp nape. She kisses him, then lays him down gently on his back. Curling into a foetal position, he falls into a deep sleep. Now Daniel is wandering through DP camps, among children with chicken-pox, in a bombed housing complex at the edge of a deep crater. The nurses, black-clad Sisters of Mercy, are cowled with guilt. Nearby an old Jewish woman spits three times at them. Daniel follows an estuary into the deeper past: stairways open beneath trap doors where Jews are hiding. He must bring them bread and water before they fall into eternal numbness.

The clangour of ice pellets against the windows roused Daniel from his dreams. In pain, he rubbed the finger-wide indentation in his left calf, where a bullet had come to rest. "Aw! Aw!" he moaned. Kathy, a short English-speaking nurse, kneaded his calf with both hands until the cramp had subsided. She sat down on his bed in the darkness and told him the story of how, as a seventeen year-old British girl, she had married a Canadian airman and came to live in Canada.

—⟫⟪—

DANIEL found himself at dawn in a small bare room with bleached popcorn walls. A sink stood next to the closed door. Above it, a metal shelf was laden with medication. A mirror hung on the wall above the shelf, its silver coating abraded along the edges. Two black iron spittoons were on the floor.

Daniel looked down from his second-floor window on the snow-covered front grounds of the hospital. Dense forest receded in all directions. Off to the right, a red tree crown stood out among the evergreens. In the distance, a pillar of smoke was uncoiling slowly into the sky. The tranquility of the scene eased the tautness on his face, and he thought: "Perhaps one day, when I'll feel stronger, I'll venture into the forest—not to hide from Germans—but to listen to the sounds of nature."

Voices from the entrance below his window directed Daniel's eyes to a horse-drawn wagon that had pulled up to the stone stairs beneath the portico. Daniel watched as a tall man, carrying a black handbag, stepped out of the wagon. He stopped to pat the horse's shoulder as if to thank it. It was a kindness that Daniel was not used to seeing. The horse seemed to appreciate it and responded with snorted puffs of mist.

A few minutes later, that same man, followed by two nurses, entered Daniel's room. Extending a friendly hand, he introduced himself: "Lucien Marquis."

Dr. Marquis held Daniel's x-ray against the window light, while one of the nurses helped Daniel sit up in his bed. The doctor proceeded to examine him: he palpated the purple contusions on his nape and back and noted the gashed forehead, the deep lesions on his shins and ankles, three missing toenails, and blistered feet. After listening to his chest, Dr. Marquis took both of Daniel's hands, helped him to his feet and observed his poor posture, his narrow shoulders bent inward. Looking into his mouth, he saw a lesion in his palate and missing molars. Seeing the blue numbers tattooed obliquely on the inside of Daniel's left forearm, Dr. Marquis couldn't conceal his horror. He stepped back from the battered body and whispered in French to the nurses, "Dogs were treated better." Returning his gaze to Daniel, the doctor asked in English: "How old are you?" enunciating each word.

Daniel understood the question, but had forgotten how to say 'twenty'. He displayed all ten fingers twice.

"Twenty?"

Daniel nodded.

"Papa? Mama?" the doctor inquired. Daniel looked askance. Moved by the young man's restrained manner, Dr. Marquis maintained a silent gaze on him, then said: "Normally I would repeat the x-ray before prescribing antibiotics, but in your case, I will start with streptomycin injections today."

"Thank you," Daniel said.

The doctor made notes, handed them to the nurse, then left the room. Daniel stepped to the window. The horse was standing under the portico, neighing patiently. Daniel went back to his bed. The horse and the wagon had conjured memories from another life.

He was six years old when a loud commotion in front of the family home woke him from his morning sleep. Men were shouting in Polish outside the house. Daniel's father had served in the Polish cavalry before his marriage. Now he was being conscripted for a year of reserve duty. All year there had been talk of war with Germany. Daniel clambered up to the high window in his room to catch a glimpse of his handcuffed father being dragged away by soldiers to a horse drawn wagon much like the doctor's. Daniel's mother and five sisters were screaming. Daniel ran out barefoot in his pajamas and chased the wagon down the main street of the village. His grandfather, a man in his seventies was also running, carrying the phylacteries his son had left behind. Grandfather stumbled to the ground. "Bring this to your father. Run! Run!" Daniel ran after the wagon, clutching the bag of phylacteries, but by the time he reached the station, the train had already left.

꧁꧂

DANIEL got out of bed in the middle of the night, wrapped a blanket over his hospital gown and stepped into the corridor. A kerosene lamp was flickering as he shuffled past the nursing station where two nurses exchanged quizzical glances at the ghostlike figure slinking silently past them. Daniel mounted the stairs slowly to the top floor, then emerged into a small ornate lobby. A wide door opened into a chapel. Between two narrow arched windows stained with biblical images stood an ark. Large silver candelabras were on small tables on either side of a podium where the Torah scroll was read.

Stepping out of the chapel, Daniel then walked down the corridor. The door to a small library was open. The outside wall of the library was constructed of glass blocks through which there was a distorted view of the moonlit forest behind the hospital. A pathology book lay on a desk. It piqued Daniel's interest. He opened it and skimmed through the pages. A plaque on a nearby wall honored Sir Mortimer Davis, the Founder and President of the Imperial Tobacco Company of Canada, for having financed the acquisition of the land on which this lung hospital was built.

Daniel then made his way to the main lobby and from there to the basement. The lighting was poor, the passageways covered with soot. A boy of twelve or thirteen, with the blackened and gloomy face of a coal miner, was shovelling coal into the red mouth of the furnace in the boiler room. Daniel gazed at him through a pall of coal dust and read the expression of misery on his face. He gestured with his hands that he wanted to help him shovel the coal, but the boy refused. In broken English, the boy said: "My father is sick."

-»€«-

DANIEL was transferred the next morning to a large room with four beds. Sunlight lit up the walls and slanted shadows of window frames latticed the grey cement floor. A middle-aged woman with disheveled hair and two middle-aged men were eating breakfast in their beds. The man in the bed adjoining the woman's, was bald, round-shouldered, with narrow eyes in a long face. A violin lay at the foot of his bed.

"Pinchus Gerlitski," he introduced himself affably.

"Edelman," Daniel whispered.

Daniel learned that Pinchus had studied Torah in the great yeshivas of Eastern Europe before the war. He fled after Germany occupied Poland, but was captured crossing into Slovakia. He escaped again and joined the Russian partisans in the Ukraine. His sharply focused look was in stark contrast to a forlorn voice entreating pity. Pinchus resembled Uncle Zushe, Daniel's mother's younger brother. Zushe had no faith in the Yeshiva system of study where all learning was oral. Taking it upon himself, he taught Daniel mathematics, which he referred to as the universal language. Daniel's father disagreed. For him, Hebrew was the holy tongue and he tried to prove it with Kabbalistic interpretations of Hebrew words. Uncle Zushe moved to Israel a few months before the war broke out. There he married an American émigré. Rumours had it that in 1941 he moved with her to New Jersey where he opened a bakery and became a successful businessman.

Daniel placed his possessions on his bed. During the move from one room to the other, he had missed breakfast. He noticed the patients had left food on their plates, which an orderly was collecting. Following him into the corridor where the trays were placed on a cart, Daniel took a piece of toast from the leftovers, mixed a half glass of orange juice with the remains of a cup of coffee and drank unabashedly. A nurse who had been observing him, offered Daniel a full glass of orange juice. The wet glass slipped through his hand and shattered on the cement floor. "Jews always bring bad luck," she muttered under her breath in French.

THAT AFTERNOON, the second man in the room approached Daniel's bed with a camera dangling over his abdomen. The pear shape of his body became fully apparent as he stood leaning slightly forward in front of Daniel.

"George," he said, extending his hand in friendship. He was a medium-sized man with a round shaven face.

The outer folds of his ears were overgrown with thick black hair. Sitting down on the edge of Daniel's bed, he launched into his story of how the atomic bomb had saved his life. George was born in the Netherlands in 1912. As a promising young photographer for a Dutch newspaper, he had been assigned to the 1936 Berlin Games. He became enamoured of German society, engraving in him a bias which in the early years of the war, exonerated Nazi atrocities. George was enlisted in the Dutch Air Force and sent to the East Indies. There he was trained as a navigator on the American Martin B-10 Light Bombers. The Japanese Zeroes shot down his plane in the first major air battle of the war. He was captured, then sent to Japan as a slave labourer in the Nagasaki shipyards. Three months before the war ended, George was transferred to the coal mines north of the city. When the atomic bomb fell on Nagasaki, he was hundreds of feet underground. Upon emerging from the mine, a plume of smoke greeted him. At first, he thought the Americans had hit an ammunition dump. A month later, George was on a ship headed to Europe. His TB was diagnosed in Amsterdam, but he concealed it from Canadian immigration officers. He arrived alone in Montreal in the summer of 1950. Now, more than a year since his admission to the hospital, there was little improvement in his condition. Deep gurgling was heard from his chest, usually an overture to a bout of heavy coughing that went on until a nurse came and slapped him unceremoniously on the back.

It was only on the second day in his room that Daniel met Sheila Weinberger. He would later learn that she was born into a wealthy Montreal family and spent a spoiled youth in high society. She was engaged in her early twenties to a wealthy young man who jilted her a week before the wedding. Humiliated, she left Montreal and began traveling with the hope of finding new love. While the Jews of Europe were being slaughtered, Sheila was dancing the nights away in the *milongas* of Buenos Aires, where she had gone to perfect her tango with the masters. There in the sleazy smoke-filled dance halls, she squandered her health and the family fortune she had inherited, and contracted TB.

⟫⟪

EVELYN Ramer came to the hospital one afternoon with her usual cheerful demeanour. She brought a valise packed with clothing. Her husband's navy suit was folded across her left arm for fear it would become wrinkled inside the valise. Daniel stood up from his bed. Without so much as a word, she measured it on him as the other patients looked on.

"Nathan had worn it only once," she said. "I might have to take the hem up an inch or two. We'll see. I have needle and thread with me so don't worry. You'll look like a million," she assured Daniel. "Go into the bathroom and try it on right away."

Evelyn waited anxiously for him to reappear. When he did, she saw at once that Nathan's suit was too large on him. The jacket lay rucked up on one shoulder like an accordion. She straightened it with a tug and a pat, looked him up and down, and pronounced a perfect fit. "The pants fit too. And I was sure they would be short. Good, good." Finally, she hung up Nathan's winter coat on a hook on the wall near Daniel's bed.

※

THOSE patients strong enough to walk, assembled in the cafeteria Friday nights for the Sabbath meal. They were served from behind a hatch. The cook, an elderly woman, a survivor of the camps, came out from the kitchen to help serve roasted chicken.

It was Evelyn's custom to help with the Sabbath meal. She tied on an apron and proceeded to feed the weaker patients. She thought Daniel looked ill and rested her tepid motherly hand on his forehead to feel if he had fever. Daniel was sitting next to Sheila, who was not in a talkative mood, nor had much appetite. She argued frequently with patients and nurses when she was not lying in bed. Though she did not cough as much as the others, her waxen face, her unkempt hair and hardened curls sticking out in all directions, made her look more ill than she was. She took a few bites of her chicken, then pushed her plate aside. Instinctively, Daniel reached out for the discarded plate and ate her leftovers. He fumbled with the cutlery when he tried to use them, so he ate with his hands instead. He sat hunched over, shovelling food into his mouth in claw-like gestures while Sheila looked on in horror.

After the patients had left the dining hall, Daniel lingered there alone, gobbling down what leftovers he could find on the plates, breaking meatless bones with his few good molars.

❧

DANIEL regained some strength by the end of the first week. One morning he donned the coat Evelyn had given him and strolled the grounds. The bright sunlight reflecting off the freshly fallen snow burned his eyes. He sought refuge in the shadows of trees along the road girdling the frozen pond. From time to time he stopped and spat blood-tinged phlegm, watching it burrow deep into the snow. He noticed garbage boxes along the side of the hospital building on the way back. Again, by force of habit, he rummaged through them for scraps of food and found withered orange peels which he quickly scoffed down. Dr. Marquis was making his way to the hospital entrance when he saw Daniel eating from the garbage. He pretended not to notice.

⟞⟝

ANITA Kreisman spent three years in concentration camps, but her zest for life and the Yiddish theatre had not diminished. She had organized clandestine performances in Bergen-Belsen to boost the morale of prisoners and to satisfy her craving to act. The theatre was for her a chapel and acting, the highest form of worship.

Anita found employment in a clothing factory soon after arriving in Montreal in 1948, though she did not stop searching for work in her beloved profession. An advertisement in the Canadian Jewish Eagle for a Yiddish teacher in the tiny Jewish community of Sainte-Agathe caught her eye. She packed the couple's meager possessions and they headed north. With Hershel in tow, she went to meet Mrs. Ramer at her home on the shores of Lake Sainte-Agathe. Before entering, Anita pinched her husband's pale cheeks to raw redness. As she looked him over, she could not understand what had drawn her to him—a despondent man with pocked cheeks, who had caught her fancy in a DP camp when she saw him applauding enthusiastically long after she had finished her performance.

The sight of Evelyn's smiling face had immediately rewarded Anita's intuition. After a ten-minute interview she was hired. The job entailed teaching children how to read and write Yiddish in a late afternoon program that would complement their regular studies in a local English school. It was far from Anita's dream of kicking up her heels on a shining stage floor, but for now it was a step forward. First she had to learn English to communicate with the children. She found a tattered copy of *Tom Jones* on a shelf in Evelyn's basement and threw herself into the novel.

⇥⟐⇤

LAUGHTER was heard on the front grounds of the hospital. It was a Sunday afternoon late in November. A troop of children had trudged through the snow all the way from Sainte-Agathe and were now making their way around the pond. Weighed down by their winter coats and heavy boots, they burst noisily into the hospital lobby.

Anita had delayed rehearsals until she suddenly realized there were only three weeks left until the Hanukah festival. To make matters worse, a snow storm had forced the cancellation of the first rehearsal. Her reputation and her job depended on the success of the performance, the first demonstration to the community that much had been accomplished with their children since she moved here in the spring.

Dr. Marquis had assured Anita that none of the patients were contagious, but this had not allayed her fears.

"Don't breathe!" she commanded the children as they made their haphazard ascent in the stairwell, holding their coats and boots in hand. Anita and Hershel ran from child to child, covering mouths and noses to prevent them from inhaling. After passing the two floors of TB patients and reaching the fourth floor, they relaxed.

Once the children were settled in the auditorium Anita shouted the dreaded words: "Time for noses!" Then she assumed her infamous akimbo stance, armed with tissues twisted to points like sharpened pencils, while Hershel stood guard at the doors to prevent escape. One by one, the children apprehensively approached the teacher with noses uplifted and Anita poked the tips deep into each nostril to scrape out any secretions and dried mucus. She was convinced that all illnesses—especially tuberculosis—invaded the body through the nose.

At last Anita was ready to start the rehearsal. She arrayed the children on stage in two rows behind six chairs. Two noses were bleeding, but that did not matter to Anita because she knew the nostrils were clean and the children were protected against TB. She ordered Hershel to attend to the children with a big white kerchief she had prepared for just such little mishaps. Hershel did as ordered, then followed Anita around the stage, a sleepwalker leashed to her hand, commiserating with her every frustration by nodding at the appropriate moments with an intensity controlled by the pitch of her voice.

"Sit down!" she commanded, grabbing the timorous Hershel by the shoulders and forcing him down onto a chair. Then, she shouted at him: "Oh, get up you silly man! I don't know you! I'm not married to you! Who are you, anyway?"

She turned to the children. "Children, children! Why is everybody playing games and talking when the teacher is thinking? Do you want this play or not? Your parents and the entire community will be so embarrassed by you as you mumble and stumble and trip all over each other on stage!" Hershel walked around pleading obsequiously with the children for silence. Anita cried in despair: "Do you want the teacher to lose her voice? Ask yourself, in the depths of your hearts! If there isn't complete silence in five seconds, then no popsicles! Not for Jordan! Not for Jeremy! Not for Alicia and not even for Heather! Final!" she blared as if these children, all from well-to-do homes, could actually be swayed by the promise of popsicles in winter. "Now you know I mean business!" She nodded vehemently as her taut face exhibited the agitation of having to resort to the ultimate threat. In a calmer voice, she said: "Children, you all know that in three short weeks you'll be wearing the uniforms Mrs. Ramer has so kindly sewn for you, but for now you must pretend you're wearing them." Bending over to a short boy, she declared: "You are Yehuda HaMaccabe and you're wearing a beautiful king's uniform with a gold crown on your head and you're holding a silver sword in your right hand. I know you don't have it in your hand at this very moment but just pretend you do. I also know you are a lefty, but there it is in your right hand. Just hold it tightly and raise your arm high!" The boy gazed quizzically at his empty hands and the invisible sword. "Now please step forward. Have you been practising your speech? Again, listen carefully to me, how I pronounce every word: 'Be brave my brothers in the war against our enemies who prevent us from serving God in our Temple. It is better to die in battle than to see the sorrow of our people and the destruction of our Temple!' Speech needs the ring of truth!" she chastised the delinquent children. As she confronted the bored expressions on their faces, she fell into a swoon. Hershel held her up on her feet as she pleaded: "Children, children! Do you want your dear, devoted teacher to die of a heart attack at the tender age of thirty-two? My birthday is next week. You all know that."

Anita was at wit's end, desperate for a semblance of order in the chaos she herself had created. The children had learned to yawn at her harangues. She felt awful. Scowling with self-inflicted misery, she regretted her uncontrollable tirade. She had not meant to berate the innocent children. How many Jewish children had already been lost in the war? How could she not love each and every one of those precious little souls? It was only that her professionalism had taken possession of her.

"Anita, please relax, it's only a rehearsal," Evelyn consoled her. "They're children and the performance doesn't have to be perfect. No one expects perfection from children. Everyone just wants to have a good time. Most of the parents don't even speak Yiddish."

"I know, I know. You're right, you're right, but I can't help myself. I'm a professional!"

"We all know that."

Anita thought, she must not give up, she must persevere as she had persevered all her life. She had survived the concentration camps and so she would survive the rehearsal.

Daniel was standing just inside the open doors, wearing a house coat and the fur-lined slippers that had belonged to Evelyn's husband. He almost forgot himself while he gazed amusedly at the pandemonium on stage, happy for these Jewish children who were enjoying their childhood.

As the rehearsal drew to an end, a young woman strode toward the auditorium in a sprightly gait. The hood of her coat lay furrowed on her shoulders, revealing glistening red hair. A wide space between her upper front teeth was a tiny setback in an otherwise beautifully dimpled face. Daniel looked directly at her as she brushed past him and made her way toward the stage. Someone shouted to one of the students: "Heather, your sister Gilla is here to take you home."

Daniel stood for a moment gazing at Heather and her sister as the crowd dispersed around him. When he returned to his room, he stepped to the window and looked down on the front grounds. The young red-haired woman he had seen in the auditorium and her sister were walking toward a large car parked near the pond. They got in and drove away under the canopy of snow-laden tree crowns.

-»)«-

THE SNOW that had been falling all morning was tapering off when Daniel left the hospital grounds on his foray into Sainte-Agathe. Along the quiet country road, the spines of snow drifts meandered smoothly, occasionally swirling into high points like topping on fancy pastry. On the side of the road, loaves of white bread capped mailboxes. A wagon lay on its side in front of a barn, a rusted wheel rim revolving slowly in the wind. Nearby, a crow stood guard on a wooden post, and further up the road there was a dilapidated shack where a toppled statue of the Virgin Mary blocked the door.

Daniel moved to the shoulder of the road when he heard a car approaching. He waited for it to pass, then stepped back onto the road now walking in the furrows the tires had left in the freshly fallen snow. The forest opened on one side and Daniel could see homes and farm houses stretching into the distance. Coppices held their cauliflower heads above the undulating fields of snow partitioned by long lines of fir trees. Splotches of cloud shadows raced silently across the vast white meadows like a herd of animals.

The road followed a river, then crossed over it along the narrow bridge Daniel had seen on his way from the train station to the hospital. He stopped on a hilltop at the entrance to Sainte-Agathe to admire the postcard scene spread out before him: colourfully dressed skaters on the lake, sleighs sliding down slopes. The village lay under a grey tarpaulin of cloud propped up by church spires, cradled on three sides by mountains. Smoke curled out of chimneys and horse-drawn sleds burrowed into hill sides. To the north, mountain tops were enshrouded in fog with varying density through which peaks appeared now and again.

Daniel noticed spittoons on the streets when he entered the village. A restaurant window displayed a sign in French: "No dogs! No Jews!" At a gas station another sign announced: "Christians only!" Evelyn had warned him about these signs and told him that it represented the views of a small minority who were concerned that Jews were bringing TB to the north.

Men sat on chairs, ice fishing in the middle of the lake. Daniel saw two young women skating, both wearing identical tight black pants and red jackets. The taller one skated far out on the lake. People were shouting at her in English from the shore: "Gilla, come back! The ice is thin in the middle." She pirouetted on the tips of her skates, then came racing to the shore, tracing a wide arc as she waved and smiled happily to the onlookers. Daniel recognized the young red-haired woman he had seen at the Hanukah rehearsal.

When the low sun appeared meekly from behind the clouds, Daniel turned back to the hospital. The cab driver who had picked him up at the train station along with Evelyn, honked a friendly hello, then passed with a wave of his arm through the open window. Daniel responded in kind.

⚜

A FLOCK of geese overhead descended stridently into the forest. Daniel followed their cries along a path sheeted with ice that shattered easily underfoot. Finally he caught sight of them through an opening among the bushes: hundreds of Canada geese resting on a frozen pond. Their heads and necks were black, faces white, bodies brown. A dead elk lay on a dock, clods of earth stuck to its antlers, a reddish hue overlaying the open eyes. Rustling sounds emerged from the bush ahead of him. Daniel saw camouflaged hunters poised on the edge of the pond, rifles aimed at the geese. The white, frostbitten lobe of a hunter's ear appeared among naked branches, his bare fingers on the trigger. Suddenly there was a fierce volley of fire and crimson-black puffs rose up from the pond. Most of the geese were slaughtered on the pond; some felled in midair, plunking through the ice, bellies up, pink intestines sprouting, floating in a cauldron of bloodied water. Another barrage of fire was followed by screeching echoing into the forest. A cackling gosling tried to take off with one wing flapping wildly. Others ran over the ice toward the wooded bluff, but were stopped short. A hunter's bloated face trembled as he blew the head off a goose. It flew on for a few seconds, then arched precipitously downward.

Wearing high rubber boots, the hunters stepped onto the ice to collect their bounty. One man picked up a goose that was still alive. He held it by the legs and swung the head repeatedly against the edge of the dock until all signs of life were gone. Blood dripped from the sky as the few surviving geese climbed above the forest, chased by violet trails of gunfire as a porous V-formation took shape in the air. One goose straggled behind the others, then caught up, co-opted into the orphaned formation high above the forest. Daniel looked at the crimson pond, his head quivering. The dead geese were full of buckshot, like pomegranates filled with seeds.

The sun had slid beneath the mountain coping and

the temperature was plummeting. Daniel saw the stucco facade of the hospital in a spray of sunlight from under clouds and hastened his pace. Rusting metal ramparts of the roof shimmered between the turrets. He plodded up the road skirting the pond, gasping. Light alternated with shadows of chestnut trees like a piano keyboard.

A nurse in the lobby noticed Daniel's trembling blue lips. She touched his forehead with her hand and was convinced he had a fever.

"You have to rest. Rest is the main part of the cure. I am sure Dr. Marquis did not give you permission to go out. I'll be speaking to him about you!" she reproved him, shaking her head with displeasure.

An orderly came after supper to take Daniel to the bathing room. The hot water was drawn and towels with singed corners hung on the back of the door. The gurgling water draining out of the tub spoke to him in a language he did not understand. Later, he noticed Sheila standing in the doorway as he was getting out of the tub. She did not apologize for the intrusion, only muttered: "I was scheduled for seven o'clock."

Daniel could not sleep that night. Lightning rent the night sky like the veins of a maple leaf.

AN EARLY December blizzard draped the hospital in heavy snow. Long spears of ice dangled dangerously from eaves. A howling wind swayed the tree crowns and stirred the bushes sticking out of the snow. At the height of the storm, the hospital was whipped with sheets of snow and ice, each lash depositing a visible layer on the grounds. Branches of willow trees creaked under the weight of ice, clinking musically in the wind. On the front grounds, large broken boughs lay in the snow, having brought down the hospital electricity lines.

The hospital ran out of coal during the second night of the storm. Road conditions had made delivery impossible. Kerosene ovens warmed the corridors, but couldn't keep up with the falling temperature. A wood-burning oven in the main lobby functioned well. Many patients gathered there, wearing coats and gloves, but the cold from the cement floors went right through their shoes. Meanwhile maintenance workers were braving the icy winds to collect fallen branches from the surrounding forest to feed the coal-burning oven in the basement. The patients were given extra blankets, but to little avail.

The kitchen depended on daily food deliveries. Men on staff were ready to go to Sainte-Agathe by horse and sleigh or even on foot to bring essentials. The nurses slept in a dormitory in a nearby building so the wards were always staffed. Many of the war survivors were convinced they would die of cold or hunger.

Daniel ventured into the portico where the snow had been blown waist high. He took a moment to savour the isolation the storm had brought before making his way into the high snow. Standing under a clear morning sky, the majestic remains of the storm spread out before him, he inhaled shallowly to prevent chest pain. Large snowflakes drifted slowly down from the trees as an old truck groaned its way up the road, sputtering to a stop in front of the hospital entrance. A heavy man with a bushy black beard emerged. Silver teeth gleamed in his ruddy face as he went about unloading crates of eggs and milk. Daniel went down to greet the man. A conversation struck up between the two of them in Yiddish. The farmer had arrived in Canada in the early thirties from Poland, settled in a village half-way between Montreal and Sainte-Agathe, and built a chicken farm. He raised a family, never compromising his religion.

Mounting the back of the truck, the farmer pulled two crates to the edge of the truck bed. The movement unnerved the chickens inside the crates. Donning a white apron, the farmer cleaned his hands with snow then drew a blade from a leather bag. Soon chicken blood was melting deep narrow tubes in the snow. He worked fast, steam puffing from his mouth and nostrils. Finished with the slaughtering, he took a handful of sawdust and sprinkled it over the blood.

The sight of a Jew slaughtering chickens kindled pangs of longing in Daniel for the *shtetl* life he had known as a child. Daniel's grandfather had been the ritual slaughterer in their community. He drank copiously at every religious occasion so his nose and cheeks were permanently flushed. On Saturday afternoons, after imbibing many glasses of whiskey, he would be accompanied home from the synagogue by two strong men as he sang Chassidic tunes at the top of his voice. For him, the Messiah had arrived.

Daniel had particularly fond memories of his grandfather who had always been kind to him. He recalled when the old man had taken him to a market in a large town when he was five or so. On the way there was an art gallery with paintings in the window displaying country scenes. In one of the paintings a train was moving through a corn field, a column of smoke rising straight up from the engine stack. As they looked at the beautiful painting, he remembered how he had cried out: "Zeidie! It's not true!" "What's not true?" his grandfather had asked. "Smoke doesn't go straight up like in the picture!" His grandfather had smiled with pride. He took the boy in his arms and promised: "You'll be a great Torah scholar one day."

※

THE ELECTRICITY was still out. To keep food cold a maintenance worker hacked ice out of the pond, then pulled the blocks up to the building in a sled. When the man reached the embankment, Daniel went down to help him pull the sled up the incline. The toothless, unshaven man croaked words of gratitude in French, then clapped Daniel on the back. Daniel followed him into the building. He noticed Sheila gazing at him. She approached him and said: "You told me that you don't know how to dance. But I entered your dream when you were sleeping and I saw you dancing. Yes, you were dancing."

"You are right," he said, full of pity for her. "Next time I will dance with you."

"You promise?"

"Yes, I promise."

Daniel made his way to the third floor library room that evening. A kerosene lamp was burning on a table near a window. About an hour later, Doctor Marquis entered and observed Daniel struggling with a chemistry book. The doctor sat down beside him and asked him a few questions. Pleased that Daniel understood the structure of orbitals, he explained in simple English how carbon-carbon bonding works. Daniel drank in the lesson eagerly. When at length Dr. Marquis stood up to leave, Daniel got up and extended his hand to him in gratitude.

"You should study for your high school diploma," the doctor suggested. "There's an English high school in Sainte-Agathe." Daniel nodded his head. Before taking leave of his patient, he asked: "How are you feeling?"

"Better, I think."

The doctor glanced at Daniel's blood spattered hospital gown.

"We'll take another x-ray soon. You should go outside on warm days. The fresh air is good for the lungs."

⁂

LATER that week, Daniel was sitting on a bench in the lobby, poring over a biology book, when a young couple entered the hospital in great distress. The woman was holding a baby in her arms. The baby was bundled in blankets, crying weakly as the mother stammered to a nurse in French: "He has high fever and doesn't drink."

The father, a simple looking man with dirty hands

and rumpled hair, stood uneasily at her side.

"This is not a regular hospital," the nurse explained. "It's only a rehabilitation facility for adults with TB. There's no emergency room and we don't even have a doctor on the premises during the night."

"We have nowhere to go," the father pleaded. "The closest hospital is in St. Jerome and the highway has been blocked by the storm."

"I'll call Dr. Marquis," the nurse said and hurried to another room.

She returned moments later with orders to treat the infant with aspirin and tepid baths. The doctor who lived only a few miles from the hospital, was on his way.

When Dr. Marquis arrived a half hour later, he went directly to the examination room where the nurse was holding the baby. He took a swab of mucus from the baby's nose, then climbed the stairs two at a time to a small room on the third floor to examine the specimen under a microscope. The tests could not identify what was wrong with the baby.

Walking with head lowered, the doctor went to meet the parents in the lobby. The nurse followed him with the baby in her arms. Daniel stood up and approached the group. The baby was writhing, foam bubbling up in the corners of his mouth. The nurse was afraid to hold him. Daniel offered to take the infant from her.

She glanced at the doctor who nodded his approval. As the anxious dialogue continued, Daniel examined the baby under a ceiling light bulb. He noticed a scratch on the baby's scalp amid the sweat soaked hair. Holding the baby to his chest, he exposed the area to Dr. Marquis with the fingers of his right hand.

"Rabies," the doctor whispered. "There are vaccines in the city hospitals."

Daniel had heard the word 'rabies' in the DP camps. Dr. Marquis asked the nurse to call the clinic in Sainte-Jovite fifteen miles north of Sainte-Agathe, but there was a hint of hopelessness in his voice. The father cowered on a bench as the mother turned away with tears in her eyes. They could not look at their dying baby.

"I'll go with horse and sled," Daniel proposed, but the doctor rejected the idea.

Daniel walked up and down the corridor, comforting the child with Yiddish tunes he remembered from his childhood. He replaced parts of the melodies with a chant that spurted spontaneously from his heart, with words of his own that pleaded with the Angel of Death to take him in place of the infant.

In the meantime, Dr. Marquis had gone to the front desk to call Montreal to see if anything could be done. He returned moments later with a forlorn look. There was nothing Daniel could do but keep singing.

Looking down at the child, he saw a subtle tremor cross the infant's face, which seemed to glow with an ashen luminosity before the infant expired in his arms. The mother saw it at once. She shrieked then fell silent. The father stuttered incomprehensibly. A nurse bent down on one knee in front of the infant and crossed herself. The doctor took the baby, covered his face with the blanket, and carried him away from the bereaved parents.

Daniel stepped into the cold night without a coat. From beneath a naked tree crown, he looked upward and saw a river and its tributaries etched darkly on the face of the full moon. Deep in the forest a wolf was howling. Daniel recalled words he had heard in the camps, how the Angel of Death is especially fond of children.

⟩⟨

THE MOON lit up Daniel's room. Pinchus and George were asleep, but Sheila lay in her bed with eyes open.

"On a night like this, we danced in the streets of Buenos Aires," she whispered. "I can teach you how to dance if only you let me. Dancing makes it easier to be happy, and when you're happy, it's easier to fall in love," she lilted, smiling with pleasant reminiscence. "Were you ever in love?" she asked. Daniel did not answer. "I understand, of course. You lived through the war."

Daniel shuffled to the window and looked down at the front grounds. Sheila stood up and followed him. She coughed a few times, then said: "I wanted to be a good tango dancer. It wasn't the dancing that was important to me, but the holding of another human being, to be tightly in the embrace of another."

"I had an older sister who was a ballerina," he said. "She danced in the streets and in the fields. Hanna was her name. She died in Auschwitz."

The ensuing silence was interrupted by a bout of Sheila's coughing. The nurses did not respond. Daniel patted her on her back until the coughing subsided.

-᠉᠁᠁᠁-

DANIEL came across Pinchus in the main lobby where the central oven was diffusing warm, fragrant air. He had taken a liking to Pinchus who spoke in parables to protect himself from the pain of the past. Without exchanging a word, Daniel merged into his stride and they walked back and forth along the corridor. Pinchus was a kind and gentle man and would have been very popular in the hospital if not for his chronic flatulence that followed him around like a skunk on a leash. The patients and even the medical staff stayed away from him.

An orderly joked that Pinchus was the only person with whom he would venture into the forest, because then he would be safe from bears. Only Daniel was not troubled by the malodours; for him the stench of decaying corpses in the camps was still fresh to his senses. Fortunately Pinchus had a sense of humour. Once he remarked self-deprecatingly: "If my flatulence continues, I'll be able to propel myself out of this hospital, then hopefully out of this world so I can live on the moon."

"I heard people say you were a Torah scholar before the war," Daniel remarked.

Pinchus smiled. "My youth was spent in endless violin practice that blanched the faces of my contemporaries and made us old before our time. Necks as thin as pencils, the jarring sounds of our miserable efforts, the desperate scraping at the rebellious strings, all fused into an image from which I recoil even now. As I grew older, I asked myself why should I bind myself in the chains of endless violin study and bother with the countless details that spell the difference between an impassioned violinist and one who merely scratches away for his own pleasure from time to time?"

Their eyes met and Pinchus was happy to see that Daniel had understood the parable.

THE WEATHER was cooperating for the festival of Hanukah. Sunday morning, the white bandages on the sun's face gradually disappeared. The roads on the hospital grounds were ploughed wide, making room for parking along the embankments. By mid-afternoon, the entire Jewish community of Sainte-Agathe had gathered in the hospital auditorium. The children were on stage, dressed in colorful costumes and eager to perform. Anita was frantic, anxiously examining each child, peering deeply into noses with one eye tightly closed. The hospital patients trickled in, many dressed in the clothes with which they had arrived at the hospital. An usher directed them to the side of the auditorium along the windows—opened to evacuate the TB germs.

The red-haired young woman Daniel had seen a few weeks earlier, sat between her parents in the front row. Her father was tall and square shouldered, with wavy silver hair. A patch of dark brown mushroom skin tags flourished on his tanned neck. Gilla stood up frequently to wave encouragement to her sister on stage.

A boy of six or seven stepped through slabs of afternoon sunlight on the stage to a small table on which there stood a candelabra with two candles. He sang the appropriate blessings in Hebrew then lit the Hanukah candles. Loud applause followed.

The children had performed flawlessly. Daniel looked on, searching for resemblances with the faces of children he remembered from the camps.

All at once, Gilla jumped onto the stage and, with outstretched arms, encouraged everyone to join her in a dance.

"*Hava nagila hava!*" she sang as she danced, linking hands with children in a large circle.

"*Let's rejoice. Let's rejoice.*
Let's rejoice and be happy.
Let's sing. Let's sing.
Let's sing and be happy.
Awake, awake, my brothers.
Awake my brothers with a happy heart."

Daniel moved toward the stage. His gaze was locked on Gilla's luminous eyes as she flitted across the stage, her long red hair lifted by the centrifugal force of her motion. The supple movements of her hips and arms fascinated Daniel as he stared, hypnotized, waiting to be noticed by her. At last she bestowed a special smile on him, beckoning him to enter the circle, leaning toward him as she flew past. Daniel flushed and refrained from entering the dance.

BEFORE leaving the hospital, Evelyn invited Daniel to her home for the last Hanukah candle lighting on Sunday afternoon. She wanted him to meet her son who would be on his way back from skiing at Mont-Tremblant.

Evelyn lived in a spacious, well-kept cottage on a slope overlooking the lake in Sainte-Agathe. A large patio stood on wooden posts facing the shore, now covered with a foot of snow. She greeted Daniel cheerfully and accompanied him inside where she took her husband's coat from him, then introduced him to Anita Kreisman and her husband. They shook hands. Anita asked him where he had been during the war.

"In the camps," he whispered.

"But you were a child then!" she exclaimed, louder than she had intended. Daniel did not reply. Anita nodded commiseratively toward the young man.

The room was filled with small talk sprouting from huddles of guests. Some were sipping wine, while everyone enjoyed the latkes smothered with sour cream. Daniel stood in a back corner, alternating his gaze from the guests to the lake where the occasional ice skater glided past the wide panorama window. The joyful ambience intimidated him. He did not know why he had come other than in the vague hope of seeing Gilla.

Evelyn's son had returned from a day of skiing, tanned from the winter sun. He was a financial advisor for a large Canadian bank and spoke about the economics of the post-war world. He tried to engage Daniel in conversation, but he spoke English too quickly. Ten year-old Heather stood nearby holding a jar in her hand, wreathing rainbow coloured soap bubbles through a circular hole in a wand as the late afternoon sunlight poured in through openings in the curtains and frolicked on the hardwood floor.

Not long after, the sun began setting behind the mountains and it was time to light the Hanukah candles. Evelyn asked Daniel to recite the blessings, but he shook his head in refusal.

A rabbi in his late thirties with a trimmed beard and blood shot eyes had come from Fredericton, New Brunswick to be interviewed for the new synagogue that was in the final stages of planning. He had arrived with his wife, who looked much younger, a beautiful woman in her twenties. She was wearing a long black wig and a dress that went down to her ankles. She sat alone in a corner, legs together, angled sideways, feet crossed delicately. Reading from a little book, she was oblivious to the people and the bustling noise around her. From time to time, the rabbi approached to ask her if she needed something, to which she would shake her head. Daniel overheard Evelyn telling a woman that Sarah, the rabbi's wife, was a graduate of the famous Gateshead Seminary in England and that her parents had been killed in the London bombings. The rabbi had escaped Vienna days before the war. As was evident from the extensive yellow stains on his fingers, he was a heavy smoker. While he talked with Evelyn, he clutched his short beard that kept slipping prematurely through his grasp. When Evelyn suggested that he light the Hanukah candles, he agreed and in a clear loud voice sang the blessings.

Gilla arrived moments later with her father. Lowering the hood of her coat, she revealed her red hair coiled up on her nape. She hung up her coat and then her father's. Sporting a short-sleeve dress, she stepped into the living room with searching eyes. Daniel noticed her at once. The graceful ease she exuded was threatening to him. He coughed, first quietly into his cupped hands, then loudly and uncontrollably. An elderly woman was troubled by the coughing. She recognized Daniel from the Hanukah play at the hospital as one of the patients.

"He has TB!" the old woman announced in an alarmed voice. "He shouldn't be here! It's contagious! Who invited him?"

Silence fell over the room as Yiddish folk music played on in the background. Evelyn strode in holding a tray of triangular delicacies filled with poppy seeds. "I invited him," she said. "Dr. Marquis assures me that Mr. Edelman is not contagious. It's our obligation to help the survivors."

"Why is he in the hospital if he isn't contagious?"

"He's not contagious!" Gilla asserted, then walked lithely across the room toward Daniel, who stiffened at her approach. Rising on her toes, she curled her arms around his neck and, ignoring the old woman's warning, kissed him on his lips. Then she wiped away the viscous phlegm on his lips with her open hand. Smiling to the guests, she skipped across the room to the front door and ran outside without her coat. Her father witnessed the scene but did not seem surprised by her actions. He continued chatting with the rabbi as if nothing had happened.

⋙⋘

DANIEL could not sleep that night. A new face had fallen into the cauldron of facial memories, mixing with those of parents, sisters, and children in the camps. For the most part, Daniel had succeeded in corralling his childhood memories into a remote corner of his consciousness. Repulsed by visions too intense for wakefulness, it was only during his sleep that these visions surfaced and the fingers of the dead scrabbled at the tangle of memories.

He had learned that Gilla was nineteen years old and had a somewhat blemished reputation. Her escapades were well-known in the Jewish circles of Sainte-Agathe. Her father was a wealthy businessman, hobnobbing in high corporate circles of New York. Her mother was an alcoholic. But none of that was important to him. By the early hours of the morning, Daniel knew that he had been infected with the sweet cyanide of love.

***

THE HOSPITAL was gripped with Christmas rituals. Decorated and lit up evergreens stood in the lobby and outside in the portico. One evening the sounds of young voices were heard outside. A group of young and old was singing Christmas carols under the guidance of a conductor's baton. Daniel was surprised to see Gilla and her sister among the singers.

Daniel registered in the English High School Program in Sainte-Agathe the first week of January that year. He was tested in mathematics and language skills and placed at the grade nine level. The principal gave him text books, told him that he did not have to attend classes, and could write the examinations in

August. Daniel understood that the principal feared he was contagious and did not want him having contact with the other students. One night while Daniel was studying in the little library on the top floor of the hospital, Dr. Marquis entered and sat down beside him. Daniel greeted him with a friendly hello.

"I have the results of your last x-ray."

"You're resistant to streptomycin. Your lungs are not improving. There's a new medication that was developed in the U.S., but isn't available in Canada yet. We'll wait another month. If there's no improvement, I'll order it."

"Thank you," Daniel replied appreciatively.

THE FOLLOWING morning, Gilla and Evelyn's daughter came to visit patients. Sandra was younger than Gilla by three years, but half a head taller. They came with shopping bags of food and clothing and went from room to room distributing fruit and cakes. On entering Daniel's room, they found George pointing his camera to the windows. Pinchus and Sheila were out. George heard the visitors, turned, and took a photograph of the two young women. Daniel stood up from a chair where he was reading to greet them. Gilla extended her hand to him and he took it, blushing. The memory of their recent encounter arched between them and they smiled. Gilla gave him a box of chocolates and a bag of underwear that Evelyn had sent. He took everything gratefully. Then Sandra went off to find Sheila. Gilla and Daniel were left standing awkwardly side by side. His pajamas were too large on him and he had to hold up the trousers to keep them from slipping down. All he needed was a safety pin.

"How is Dr. Marquis?" Gilla asked.

"He is fine," Daniel replied.

"He helped us a lot when my older brother had his accident."

"Accident?" Daniel queried.

"Motorcycle. On the highway."

"Oh?"

"He was killed on the highway."

"Sorry to hear this."

"Five years ago." She averted her eyes and glanced down at a notebook he had placed on his bed. "Oh, is that your diary?"

"What is a diary?"

"A notebook where a person writes about everything that happens in his or her life. I keep a diary."

"I have to write an essay on Christopher Columbus for an English high school course."

"I can help you."

"Mrs. Ramer said she will help me," he said, but nodded thankfully, donned his housecoat, and accompanied Gilla to the exit on the ground floor where Sandra was waiting. Their hands touched as they walked side by side.

Daniel asked: "At the Hanukah party... How were you so sure I was not contagious with TB?"

"I wasn't sure. But if you were contagious, I would have been very happy."

"Why?" he asked incredulously.

"Then we'd be in the hospital together. Maybe even in the same room."

"You're a funny girl," he remarked.

"Some people say that," she said with a smile.

FOUR asbestos miners from Eastern Quebec arrived at the hospital in the back of an open truck in the middle of the night. Nurses in overcoats were waiting for them in the portico and ran down the slippery steps to help them. The emaciated men could hardly walk. They were dying of an unknown lung disease.

DANIEL concentrated on his studies over the next weeks. Late one afternoon, needing a break from his books, he strolled with George towards Sainte-Agathe. Snow covered outcroppings of rock, spread downward onto the embankments like the paws of polar bears. The gargoyle shadows of trees extended onto the fields. As they walked silently together, Daniel recalled the exact moment in the camps when he had decided to stop talking. From then on he lived instinctively from one moment to the next, like a hunted animal, without any expectations. He justified his behavior with words his father had once told him: "Wise men don't need to talk; their speech comes from the deepest level of the soul, and there words are unnecessary."

Overhead the sky became entirely clear, but to the west a mushroom cloud rose above the forest. Every once in a while George spat blood copiously into the snow on the side of the road.

"This is how it must have looked when I was underground," George observed phlegmatically, haunted by the bomb. After some moments he asked rhetorically: "Why was I underground when the bomb fell? I often think it would have been better if I had been above ground. If saving my life was God's wish, what was the purpose of it? I've accomplished nothing with my life. I never married and have no children. Now I'm dying of TB. What was the purpose of my existence—to leave behind a few photographs?"

⁂

IT WAS sometime in March. Daniel sat studying in a corner of the main lobby. Dusk turned into night as he made do with whatever little light he had from an overhead window. Soon he was sitting in darkness. He laid his head down and dozed off. Hours later, he was awakened by the sounds of a woman crying. Looking up from within the shadows that hid him, he saw Gilla walking slowly between her mother and Dr. Marquis, who seemed to be holding her by the elbows. Her mother was sobbing. Gilla's face was pale and expressionless. As they crossed the lobby toward the entrance, Dr. Marquis said: "In a few days you'll be entirely healed." Daniel did not know if the doctor had said this to Gilla or to her mother. A taxi was waiting for them below the portico. Dr. Marquis helped the women into the back seat and the taxi drove off into the darkness.

⁂

WINTER finally loosened its grip on the north in early April. The snow was melting on mountain slopes, leaving only a few white trails. But in shadows of the hospital facade, snow was still piled up on the arms of summer chairs shaped like boxes. Hospital workers were gathering winter debris into large heaps to be burned later. Daniel was strolling the grounds as he was wont to do on pleasant days. A stately tree near the nurses' residence had drawn his attention. Within the crown, a nest was perched among the naked branches like a tumour in a brain. Standing in the shade of the tree, he heard the rhythmic clangour of a galloping horse on the cobblestoned driveway circling the pond. Daniel looked through the wavy air rising over a bonfire and saw Gilla on a russet horse at the bend where the country road turned into the hospital grounds. She continued up the road, greeting workers on the way. Then reaching the portico, she leapt to the ground, tied the horse to a bench and slid the knapsack she had been carrying off her shoulders. The patients were familiar with the treats she brought them.

Daniel went back to the portico and stood behind a group of patients, a head taller than the others, while Gilla distributed pastries, Coca-Cola bottles and fruit. She stepped between two women and handed Daniel a wrapped bag, which he accepted with a grateful nod. After an exchange of demure glances, Gilla mounted the horse and clucked it into a trot down the slope, vanishing behind the trees along the road to Sainte-Agathe.

-⁂-

DANIEL looked down at the burgeoning green on the front grounds from his room window and imagined he was a bystander to an argument. After an exchange of shouting, one of the disputants hurled a final insult, then stomped away in a huff. And so it seemed to be with the seasons. Winter and spring had wrestled all of April. The hospital pond had been unable to decide whether to congeal or to melt and on the last day of the month, winter dumped a foot of heavy wet snow, followed immediately by a warm spell during which most of the snow melted. All that was left were dirty sloughs of snow squirming abjectly behind trees.

The sun shone unabashedly all day now. Two weeks after the last snowfall, spring was flaunting its colours like a peacock in heat. Cherry trees blossomed and mountain streams babbled incessantly. The forest floor was covered with brown cones, and the country side, fenced by fast flowing brooks, was starkly green.

Spring's arrival was marked at the hospital by an

orderly going from room to room opening windows. The sills between the inside and outside panes had become graveyards during the long winter for last summer's flies. Now the sounds of birds warbling on the roof parapet streamed in with cool refreshing air. Fresh breezes lifted papers from bed stands and floated them across rooms. At night, the silence of the forest was fractured by the cries of animals.

One morning the song of a cardinal awakened Daniel from a rare deep sleep. He looked through the open window to see a necklace of fog on the mountain facing the hospital. Two full grown deer emerged silently from the mist on the front lawn. The animals stared imperturbably at each other across the placid pond, then retreated slowly into the forest.

Unable to resist, Daniel set out for a stroll after breakfast. Maintenance men were spreading black earth over flowers beds. They yanked weeds from the soil, clods of earth clinging to the roots like memories of a dying man. Shadows of chestnut trees glistened on the glossy surface of the pond, rippling slowly. Daniel noticed a fallen nest on the flattened grass near the pond. One egg was cracked open and a dead fledgling lay nearby with its tiny beak caught in the viscid yellow mixture. Clouds of black flies followed Daniel along the country road. A wind swayed the high grass and set tree crowns into delightful motion. Balls of cotton pollen floated down from the awakening trees and covered the fields with fluff. The smell of lilac and freshly cut grass suffused the grounds. Daniel was dazzled by the deep verdure of spring and the concerto of rivulets gurgling in gullies along the road like a contented infant on her back. Even the deserted hovels with collapsed wooden roofs were alive with plant growth all around them. But at the crossroads, a tall dead birch clad in white shrouds stood guard, branches ready to claw at pedestrians. Further down the road, flat meadows of dandelions, like a leopard's skin, were bathed in sunlight. Squinting, he made his way to the shadows of the forest ahead where he would find reprieve from the deluge of light. He was wont to walk the hospital grounds, especially at dawn and dusk. One evening, after climbing a path along the facing mountain, he came upon an opening in the forest. Looking down at the hospital in the bright evening sunlight, he saw a medieval white castle, inhabited by the dispirited remnants of a cursed generation of Jews.

-⟫⟪-

DANIEL'S studies had progressed greatly by spring. He had mastered the basics of English grammar and had committed to memory a vocabulary of a few hundred words. The middle of his day was devoted to studying mathematics and biology. He was surprised how well the strict and challenging training he had received as a child in Bible studies, had prepared him for science and the rigors of mathematics. His friendship with Dr. Marquis had also blossomed. The doctor would sometimes accompany Daniel on his walks around the grounds. Daniel learned that the doctor's wife suffered from a debilitating neurological disease. One evening they walked to the highway leading to Sainte-Agathe. The doctor explained how the road was first built with trees. When the new highway replaced it, they found those logs—more than a hundred years old now—perfectly preserved, a fact that amazed the doctor. The doctor also answered a question that Daniel had not asked. Pointing to an anti-Semitic sign on a telephone pole, he said: "Most of my adult life I have fought TB in the north. It has been a difficult war, but even more difficult has been the war against the ignorance of my own people and the Catholic Church that teaches them to hate Jews."

DANIEL had heard about McGill University's famous medical school from Dr. Marquis. On a cloudless day late in April, he set out for Sainte-Agathe to ask

Evelyn if she would request application forms from the admissions office at McGill University. He went directly to the lake from the hospital and followed the gravel road around it on the outskirts of the village. The scents of blossoming trees were invisible pathways in the air. It was these invisible pathways he was seeking, when in the distance he saw someone standing in a row boat, struggling to dock against the waves. As he approached, he recognized Gilla and saw that her boat was clenched in the antlers of a sunken tree. Gilla's lustrous red hair was slicked down, dripping, the wet robe clinging to her, exposing the contours of her body.

"The boat is stuck! Please help me!" she pleaded.

Daniel stepped from boulder to boulder until he reached the boat's helm. He rolled up his trousers, slipped out of his shoes and socks, and waded into the cold lake. Standing waist high in the water, he ordered her: "Sit! Sit!" Then he began alternately pushing and pulling the boat. With one strong push the boat lurched backwards. Gilla, who was still standing with oar in hand, toppled into the lake. He clasped her hand and helped her climb back into the boat, then hoisted himself up after her. Her exposed shoulders were sprinkled with freckles. There was a bath towel on the front seat of the boat. As she reached for it, her drenched robe fell open in front, exposing her breasts. A thick scar slanted from her collar bone down across the right breast, covering the nipple.

Daniel coughed, carefully directing the phlegm into the lake, then squeezed the water from his trousers below the knees.

"You'll come to my house. My brother's clothes will fit you," she said, grasping the oars.

Gilla's bare feet pushed against the wood stop on the floor of the boat as Daniel faced her from the back bench, grasping the sides for stability. As she leaned back, digging the oars into the lake, her thin legs slightly apart, the towel slipped up high over her thighs and he saw she wasn't wearing underwear.

"Why are you in a boat by yourself?" he asked in a disapproving tone.

"I always go boating by myself."

She rowed smoothly and swiftly. Noticing the numbers on his forearm, she looked askance.

"Dr. Marquis told my mother you want to be a doctor," she said, a sensuous smile now on her lips.

"We talked about it. I am not sure."

The shadow of a solitary cloud followed them as the boat glided over the water, following the shoreline. Gilla pointed out Jewish hotels perched on the hills above the lake road, still barricaded against the winter.

"That's Lakeside Inn over there and further up the side of the mountain is the Four Leaf Clover Hotel.

In the summer they're packed with vacationers from Montreal and New York. For two months, Sainte-Agathe is a Jewish city. I love the summers here."

"What do they do here?" he asked.

"The men play cards on the patios and the women go down to the beach with the children. They swim and sunbathe."

"I can row if you like," he proposed.

"I like rowing. We're almost at my house. You'll meet my mother. Heather is in school and my father is on business in New York as usual."

Gilla secured the boat to a post at the corner of a dock, then stepped onto the deck. Daniel stood up, his soaked pants pulling on his waist. She offered him her hand to help him onto the dock, but he persevered and managed to get out himself. She walked barefoot up the grassy slope to a three storey villa with a large terrace facing the lake. Daniel followed her under the terrace and into the basement through a side door. Gilla showed him her brother's repaired motorcycle in the garage, then lead him to her bedroom, a large dimly lit room with a bed and sofa. A small desk stood under the window with a wood carving of a fisherman, pipe in mouth, serving as a lamp stand. Sunlight peeked in through the vertical edges of the shuttered windows.

The main floor had high stucco ceilings and was

bright with sunlight pouring in through large windows on three sides. A living room with a fireplace and cushioned sofas all around dominated the floor. To the side of the kitchen, a carpeted staircase ascended to the bedrooms. A back screen door opened from the kitchen to a garden and a swimming pool. A car stood in the driveway facing the street, the sun glinting off the chrome bumpers. The road girdling the lake passed behind a row of high, well-trimmed bushes.

Gilla changed into shorts and a loose sleeveless top. She brought Daniel a pair of pants, but he preferred to wear his with the wet legs rolled up. They sat at a table in the back garden where Gilla had placed blueberry pie and lemonade. Gilla's mother, a weary-looking woman in her late forties, appeared in the garden wearing a flowery smock and sandals. She was smoking a cigarette. An odour of liquor followed her as she greeted Daniel with an outstretched hand. She resembled the peasant women who used to work the fields near his *shtetl*. The woman touched her forehead as if to ease a headache and went back upstairs.

Daniel saw the disarray the house was in. "When does your father come here?" he asked.

"Weekends, sometimes."

"What does he do?"

"He's a metal dealer. He buys and sells scrap

metal in large quantities. He's embarrassed to bring us to Montreal. I think his family never approved of his marriage to my mom. She was not Jewish before they got married. My grandfather came here in the thirties with TB. When my father came to visit him, he fell in love with one of the nurses working in the hospital. My mom. She converted to Judaism. Rabbi Steinman in Montreal did the conversion, but the family said he was a fake rabbi."

Daniel wanted to enquire further. "It must be lonely for your mom here without your father," he remarked. "How do you keep busy during the days?"

"I help my mother and my sister. When I have time I study a correspondence program to become a secretary. I like to write. Especially in my diary."

Daniel stood up. "They're waiting for me at the hospital."

As they made their way up to the road, their hands touched. Wondering if it was intentional, she glimpsed at Daniel's face. "When will we meet again?" she asked when they stopped at a crossroad.

"I'm studying for the high school matriculation exams."

"All the time?"

"No, not all the time."

She took his hand awkwardly and kissed it.

-»)€«-

THE CLOYING scent of cow manure from the surrounding farms wafted across the quiet country road assailing Daniel on his way back to the hospital. A horse and wagon had stopped for no apparent reason at a railroad crossing. The scene overwhelmed Daniel with memories of *shtetl* life and he burst into tears. He had been the pampered little jewel of the family. On his seventh birthday his mother cuddled him, and his sisters took turns smothering him with kisses. Daniel stood up on a chair and promised to shoot the Polish soldiers who had taken his father away.

His mother said: "Sha, you mustn't talk like that."

"But I mean it, Mama."

"Even so, such words should never leave your lips."

-»)€«-

DANIEL walked to town Saturday evening with the intention of visiting Evelyn to discuss his plans for the fall and hopefully to run into Gilla. He arrived in Sainte-Agathe as the sun was setting. Hearing music coming from the train station, he approached. The sounds of laughter and carousing grew more distinct. Peering through a window, he saw a crowd of young people dancing on the floor, where the benches had been pushed aside to create a large open space. An old swarthy man was playing an accordion, beer suds sprinkled his stained yellow moustache. Tendrils of tobacco dangled from the rim of a pipe clenched between rotten teeth. In the middle of a large circle, a young woman was dancing zestfully as men wearing red lumber jackets and heavy boots whirled her around. She carried on a good-natured banter with them between dances, slapping one man playfully across the cheek and reprimanding another who had purposely brushed his hand across her chest. As a new dance started up and the woman chanced to come close to the window behind which Daniel stood, he recognized with shock that it was Gilla. For a moment he could not believe his eyes. Her head was tottering and she looked drunk, dancing with an intoxicated young man. As they staggered around the floor, the young man drew Gilla toward a door that opened onto the dark train platform.

Aiming an angry gaze at Gilla, Daniel strode into the hall. She continued dancing amid the boisterous tumult, failing to notice Daniel glaring at her. When she finally glanced in his direction, she met an admonitory scowl of condescension. Releasing her partner, she stepped outside the dancing circle which continued without her. The music stopped abruptly as Gilla approached him.

"Did you come to dance?" she asked him, embarrassed by his presence.

"No," he shook his head, looking sternly at her. "I want to take you home," he said, extending his hand to her.

"I was just dancing," she answered defensively, now acutely aware that he was disappointed in her.

Gilla's dancing partner stepped up to Daniel, spat on the floor, rubbed his hands together, then pushed him roughly backwards, muttering offensive words in French. Raising his fists, he prepared to strike Daniel, who did not flinch. He ignored the man, his right hand waist high in the air, open toward Gilla. All at once another man stepped between them. Daniel recognized the father of the infant who had died in his arms at the hospital. He told the crowd what Daniel had done for his dying son and demanded that no one touch him. The would-be assailant looked around for support, but finding none, backed off. Gilla took Daniel's outstretched hand and they stepped out of the hall into the darkness.

They walked in silence through the snow-covered streets, Gilla lagging a step or two at his side. She thought he wanted her to feel disgraced. He had no claim on her, but she was happy that he thought he did.

At length Daniel said: "You're drunk." She smiled and he was annoyed by the lighthearted manner in which she acknowledged his accusation.

"I'm happy you came to take me home," she said.

"You don't belong there."

"I really don't like going there."

"So why do you go?"

"Nothing better to do," she replied, shrugging her shoulders

Daniel shook his head unhappily, convinced that the young men of the village were plundering Gilla's body. By the time they reached her house on the lake road, she had sobered up.

"Thank you for walking me home," she lilted, standing on her toes for no apparent reason.

"Why are you standing like that?" he asked.

"I want to kiss you."

She ran up to him on her toes like a ballerina and kissed him on the lips, then darted toward the gate to her home garden. She turned abruptly and threw him another kiss, then skipped back to him, her smile brimming with intimacy.

"I feel you're angry at me. Please don't be, dear Daniel. I love you." She blurted out these words, then kissed him again.

For Daniel, each kiss reminded him of a final parting at a train station. By the time he reached the hill where the highway intersected the country road to the hospital, Daniel thought that perhaps Gilla's presence at the dance hall was not sufficient proof that she led a decadent life. Perhaps this was how young Canadians innocently spent Saturday nights.

The late evening sun cast shadows of the mountains over the town and on the silky surface of the sleepy lake. With its long inlets marked out by street lamps, the lake became a bejewelled hand in the middle of a village that had become far more complex than Daniel could have ever imagined.

⁂

THE HOTEL staff began arriving mid-June. The cooks were elderly women survivors, and the waiters were Canadian-born medical students. Many guests arrived by train from Montreal, clutching children as they trekked across town toward the lake, looking much as they did in the DP camps with their scruffy clothing and battered luggage. The wealthier guests arrived in cars, among them men wearing white pants or Bermuda shorts. The hotel parking lots were full with cars sporting New York license plates.

The card players wasted no time in ensconcing themselves on the patios that faced the lake. The rotten wooden planks on the decks groaned under the weight of the satiated guests. The poker games started mid-afternoon and continued late into the night with religious fervor. Laughter sprouted here and there, but it often seemed contrived, and could not entirely dispel the memories of war drifting over the tables. The heaviest smoker was a Mr. Gold, no more than five feet tall. He played standing up, but it appeared to all as if he was sitting like the others. Waiters accumulated credit for future tips by serving cake and coffee well past midnight.

⟞⟋⟍⟝

GILLA came to the hospital one day and made her way to Daniel's room, where he was lying in bed studying physics. Only Sheila was in the room with him.

"Have you forgotten me?" she asked diffidently, standing at a distance and looking charmingly innocent, her hair arranged in two long pony tails which she carried on her shoulders like a scarf.

Daniel sat up.

"I am not sure," he said with a genial smile. Gilla's giggle disturbed Sheila, who turned her back to the couple.

"Evelyn suggested I take you for a walk."

"Excellent idea," he agreed at once.

They left the grounds of the hospital and walked toward Sainte-Agathe. A bright warm sun shone through open blue sky between an armada of small white edged clouds. Gilla darted in front of him, pirouetting with childlike joy. They came to a small foot bridge that straddled rapids. Daniel stopped in the middle and looked down on the gurgling water.

"In the camps, religious Jews used to sing, *The whole world is a narrow bridge—the main thing is to have no fear,*" he whispered reflectively. "They believed they would survive. A few did."

"After my brother died, I lost my fear of everything," Gilla said. They walked on in silence for some moments, then she asked: "Do you remember your sisters?"

"A little bit. There were five of them. All older than me."

Except for a few childhood memories, Daniel remembered his sisters only from his father's stories in the camps.

"It must be very painful. If you're able to talk, I'd love to listen. I wish I had known your family, then I would know you better."

"When the SS officers came to take our family away, one of my sisters, Ruth, ran into the corn fields. They chased her. Three shots rang out. She was my oldest sister and already married."

"Oh no," Gilla gasped. "I wish I had been there instead of her," she said impetuously. "I mean it with all my heart. I would have loved to have been there with you."

Daniel and Gilla found themselves in a grassy rectangular field. At one corner stood a section of a stone chimney that had served the fireplace of a house.

"I was a child when this house burned down," she said wistfully. "I remember people talking about the fire department refusing to respond to repeated calls. Everyone knew that this mansion was owned by a rich Jewish businessman in Montreal."

They came to a stand of birch whose shadows formed a panel fence across the foot path in front of them. Gilla stood in the sunlight between the shadows, her face directed to the sun.

"I love light!" she exclaimed joyously.

"I like the darkness in shadows. I like to walk through shadows slow," he said, sharing with Gilla what he deemed to be a deep truth about himself.

"Not slow, slowly," she corrected him smilingly. "The sentence needs an adverb. It sounds funny otherwise." She tried to hold back a laugh.

"Is my English so funny?" he objected.

"No, not really. Sometimes I laugh for no reason. Mostly when I'm happy. Now I'm happy." Then she burst into laughter so hard, that she bent over and urinated. "I'm absolutely soaked!" she laughed, looking down at her white socks that had turned dark. "Whenever I laugh like that I pee. I can't control myself. Then I have to walk bow legged until my undies dry."

A puddle lay on the earth between her dusty shoes. She reached under her dress for her panties, pulled her shoes through the openings, then flung it into the forest. Daniel was no longer surprised by anything she did.

They came to a foot path that followed the railroad tracks through a forest to Sainte-Agathe.

"Did you ever think of the meaning of love?" she wondered. "To me, you love a person when you're not aware of the other person," she said. "The other person becomes like your own body."

"To me love means the creation of more loss because whomever you love, you will eventually lose."

"I'm not sure of that," she disagreed politely.

"There's a curtain between people that blurs everything enough for them to fall in love and get married and have children. But survivors like me, they tear away the curtain right at the beginning. They see the ugly end before the beautiful beginning because they have already lived the end."

Gilla looked up at him empathetically. "I don't want to hide anything from you," she said. "So I'm happy you saw my scarred breast." He did not want to admit that he had seen it. "I'm sure you did. I saw your face. You were disgusted."

"I don't know what you're saying—I was not disgusted at all," he responded, refusing to agree with her perception.

"I want to tell you what happened."

"You don't have to."

"I want to. For my sixth birthday party, my mother had a beautiful pink dress hand-embroidered for me, with lots of silky material all around. I blew out most of the candles on the birthday cake, but not all. One of my friends tried to help, but unintentionally blew the candle flame directly onto me. In a second, my dress was up in flames. Before my mother could pull the dress off, my chest was burned."

"I'm so sorry," Daniel said compassionately.

"At least I have one good side," she said with a shrug of resignation. "I pray that if I ever have a baby, I'll be able to nurse."

"Of course you will," he reassured her.

"Thank you. You're very sensitive and kind, but you know the truth."

They emerged on a hill overlooking the hotels. Nearby, scattered daffodils grew on grassy hillocks. Gilla pointed out a dwarf tree, its trunk bent knee high at ninety degrees.

"Before Heather was born, my father used to bring my brother and me here. We called it the 'horsey tree'. We bounced up and down on the wooden saddle as the horsey galloped though the forest. A few years ago my father bought two racing horses and a stable in Val David. I came to the hospital on one of those horses."

They walked on through the forest. Not far from them on a low tree branch over the side of the path, a bird was crouching over her chicks in a nest. Daniel stopped to observe.

"What are you thinking?" Gilla asked in a quiet, respectful voice.

"Nothing," he replied.

"Did the Nazis do those awful experiments on you in the camps?" she asked.

"No."

"Evelyn told me that Anita can't have children. They did those experiments on her. She hopes to adopt. They so much want to have children."

Daniel nodded in commiseration.

It was dark when they came out of the forest behind the hotels. Summer auroras were mirrored on the black surface of the lake. In the clearing sky, two vertical strips of white cloud draped the full moon in a judge's wig. Gilla looked up at the starlit sky.

"When I was a little girl," she said, taking his hand in hers.

"And when was that?" Daniel quipped, feeling more at ease then he ever remembered.

"A year ago," she laughed boisterously, then corrected herself: "Seriously, I must have been six or seven. My grandmother came up from Montreal to stay with us for the summer. We spent a lot of time together. My father was her only child. She came to Canada from Russia at the turn of the century. One night we walked around the lake. The sky was full of stars like tonight. She told me that when she was a little girl in Russia, her grandmother told her that when non-Jewish kings die they become stars in the sky. That's why Jewish girls are allowed to marry them."

"There is no connection between stars and Jewish girls marrying gentile kings," Daniel demurred, shaking his head.

"But Queen Esther married a non-Jewish king," she refuted.

"That was an exception."

"Sometimes the exception is the rule."

He thought for a moment then asserted awkwardly: "A Jewish girl like you must marry a Jewish boy like me."

She lowered her eyes and was silent, but her heart was pounding with joy. When she looked up she could not conceal a blissful glimmer in her eyes.

As they approached her house, Daniel felt a need to alleviate himself from a thought that had troubled him since that Saturday night at the dance hall.

"I'm only a few years older than you, but I feel that we belong to different generations. I don't understand your world, the beer and the dancing, and you can't understand my life, the war and the concentration camps where I grew up."

"So we should not even try to understand each other?" she probed fretfully, testing his interest in her.

"No, no. We must try," he said, nodding his head.

They arrived at her home, tired and happy at the end of a long summer day. She stood at her door, smiling, waiting. She pushed back strands of her hair that had come loose over her eyes and parted her lips. His heart beat quickly as he leaned forward and kissed her.

DANIEL noticed waiters eyeing Gilla lewdly when they visited hotel cafés together. He observed her responses. She showed no sign of enjoying their dissolute ogling and banter. Only Isaac Levy, a short curly haired medical student who whistled liturgical tunes most of the day, showed no interest in Gilla. This was Isaac's third summer working in the hotels as a waiter. He was entering his last year of medical school at McGill University. Late one morning Isaac visited the hospital to discuss the possibility of doing his residency with Dr. Marquis. There he saw Daniel in the library and took a liking to him. Daniel asked him questions about medical school, then the conversation turned to the card players and their passion for poker which intrigued both young men. Isaac alleged that the survivors were merely parlaying their prewar religious zeal to poker. He claimed that playing cards and praying involved the same mental process. Daniel did not agree and suggested there was a connection between card playing and the war experiences.

-)(-

THERE was a sudden downpour on a very humid afternoon. It was as if the church spires had ripped open the dark canvas of cloud holding back the rain. Daniel was in a hotel lobby waiting out the rain when Gilla ran in soaked from head to foot. A waiter gave her a towel and Daniel held her shivering body, then helped her dry her hair. After the rain subsided, Daniel walked Gilla to her home. She was wearing a black bathing suit, a towel on her shoulders like a scarf, her feet in sandals. Gilla's mother was asleep and Heather was out cycling with friends. Daniel sat with Gilla on the dock, their bare feet in the cold lake. He rested his arm on her shoulder and they talked about whatever came into their minds: Daniel about his sisters, especially the giggling twins he had adored and his sister Hanna who at the age of fourteen, already showed great promise as a ballerina. Gilla talked about her brother whose exploits she had admired as a child. Then she spoke about her father who lived a secret life travelling all over the world, purportedly on business. It felt strange for Daniel to be sitting in the bright sunlight in shorts and bare-chested, sunbathing, while his family lay rotting in the earth. He was ashamed of himself as he thought of their fate, while Gilla leaned affectionately against him.

June 24.

THE NIGHT of the Quebec National Holiday was delirious with fireworks. The initial sounds of gunfire threw the hotel guests into panic. Crouched and terrified, they ran frantically for safety. Many were convinced that the Germans had returned. Not even the amused smiles of seasoned staff and old guests assuaged the fear that history was repeating itself.

※

ANITA'S summer contract with the hotels included organizing the Friday night entertainment. The entire Jewish community of Sainte-Agathe and the healthier patients of Mount Sinai were invited to the first event on the beach. Gilla was overjoyed to see Daniel standing at her door, holding two bouquets of lilacs he had cut from hospital trees, a purple one for Gilla's mother and a white one for her. Gilla was wearing a short blue skirt, matching blouse, and a sombrero hat. They walked hand in hand along the lake road toward the hotels. As they approached, the sounds of laughter and song grew ever louder. Bonfires were lit on the beaches and waiters tossed branches into them. As dusk settled, the lambent light of the fires flickered on the tips of tranquil waves. Dusk was replete with hungry mosquitoes and merriment. As the guests made their way down the sandy paths to the beach, they saw the lake sprawled before them, a crucible in the mountains' embrace. Row boats splashed softly along the shore and songs of the Russian partisans sprouted up from around the bonfires.

Wearing an assortment of hospital attire, Mount Sinai patients mingled with the hotel guests. In the open fresh air, no one was worried whether they were contagious or not. A tall, middle aged man, who had served in the Israeli Army during the War of Independence, was playing a mandolin, tinkling poignantly in the darkness. Peaches, plums, and grapes shipped in from Ontario, were being served generously in large bowls.

Anita had planned a medley of Yiddish songs. She began with *Oifn Pripitchik*: '*On the hearth burns a small fire and inside the cabin it is hot, and the rebbe is teaching little children Aleph, Beis.*' She then sang the romantic melody, *Tumbalalaika*: '*A young man is deep in thought, who he should take and who not to embarrass.*'

The familiar songs wafted up from the beach to the hotel patios. One by one, the card players left the tables and made their way down to the shore, crossing the road, where moths were in delirious frenzy around street lamps. The rabbi and his wife were walking silently along the road. Her hair was covered with a long kerchief and the rabbi wore a black felt hat that attracted a cloud of mosquitoes. There was a thick black silk sash tied around his waist. The couple strolled sedately along the road. To everyone they encountered, the rabbi wished, 'A good Sabbath to you,' and smiled affably, even though they were desecrating the holy day.

Gilla and Daniel sauntered away from the beach, settling on a hilltop overlooking the scene below. The fugitive moon peeked out from behind a cloud to show Gilla's silhouette etched into the darkness. Along the shoreline, sparks of light glinted along the edges of toppling waves, gently rocking boats. Daniel acknowledged the memories summoned by the songs drifting up from the beach. He looked at Gilla, her lips quivering in deference to those memories, and her commiseration made him realize how beautiful she was.

"I must tell you something," she whispered in a confessional voice. "It's been bothering me. That night when you saw my mother and me in the hospital," she whispered, then paused and looked solemnly into Daniel's eyes. "I saw you sitting in the darkness. I want to tell you but I'm afraid you won't want to see me ever again."

"I don't want to know. It doesn't matter," he said, afraid to sully the precious moment. Gilla leaned tearfully against his shoulder. Around them fireflies were unzipping the black dress of night. He lowered his head and kissed her on the lips. She was soft and pliant in his embrace. Behind them a breeze in the forest sounded like a wind instrument. Gilla's face was radiant with anticipation. He kissed her again, gently at first, then with passion.

"I made a promise to my father," he said, then hesitated, thinking how to express the thought he had never formulated in words. "I promised that, if I survive,

I would never be happy."

"You were only a child then."

"A fifteen year old in the camps is not a child."

"If it was me, I would have promised my father to always be happy," she said. "My grandmother once told me that promises are made to be broken."

"I'm not like that," he asserted. "A word is a word. A promise is a promise."

After the performances on the beach had ended, the guests walked casually up the sandy pathways to the hotels. There was calm in Daniel's voice as he talked to Gilla about the camps. She responded with compassion and he was pleased that she cared to know what he had lived through. He lowered his lips to hers and kissed her with confidence and desire. She drew him down to her on the grass. He lifted her blouse and slipped his hand under her brazier to caress her left breast. She moved his hand to the other side so he would feel the thick scar, to test him if he would be repulsed by it. In a voice full of kindness, he whispered: "Both are the same to me."

"I love you," she murmured. "From the first moment I saw you in the hospital I have been thinking only about you, waiting for you to notice me."

In the sultry summer night, Gilla pulled her blouse over her head, then slipped out of her skirt and lay naked on the grass. As he straddled her body Daniel wrestled with images of the final march from Buchenwald. Almost at once, he fell to her side on top of his dying father. He lay on him to keep him from freezing to death. The dying man's hand emerged from beneath Daniel and raked the muddy snow, then came to rest. Daniel dug a grave in the frozen earth with his bare hands and buried his father as German soldiers looked on, discussing whether they should kill him or not. One of them said: "The Russians are collecting evidence." Daniel thought that they must have known the Biblical law forbidding the slaughter of an animal and its offspring on the same day. Daniel turned to Gilla and murmured: "My father does not let me touch you. I'm sorry. I'm sorry. I hear movements. There are Germans in the forest."

"Sh, sh," she consoled him, her eyes full of sympathy. "There are no Germans here. Everything is fine. I love you. I love you."

"I love you too," he whispered.

"You feel guilty for being alive."

"A moment ago I felt as if my soul was leaving my body."

"I love you."

"I'm afraid of getting close to you," he said.

"Why?" she asked, her eyes raised pitifully.

"Because I know I will lose you."

"You will never lose me."

"There will be another war," Daniel said.

"We have to pray that there won't be."

"I don't believe in prayers."

Gilla sought his eyes and asked thoughtfully: "So we have to continue suffering forever? What is our crime for which we have to suffer so much?"

"Our crime is being alive."

Hidden in the high grass, they fell asleep in each other's arms, a Moebius strip of limbs.

The warbling of birds roused Daniel from his sleep. In the dim light, he saw gossamer tents of dew spread across the hillside, a military encampment. Overhead, droplets stretched by gravity dangled from the tips of leaves, pearl earrings that fell and burst open on the grass. Thunderous skies champed in the distance, like dogs behind a fence.

Gilla's breathing was imperceptible amid the sounds of the awakening forest. Daniel gazed at her naked body, at a freckle slightly off center in the hollow of her back and at little veins on her thighs, blue minnows at the surface of a white aquarium. She slept on her side, so still he had to touch her and wait to feel life. The sight evoked images of naked bodies heaped up in the camps. His memory went back further to the morning before *Yom Kippur* in 1939, when as a boy of nine, he rose before dawn to stand next to his father as he twirled a chicken over the boy's head in the annual ritual of *kaporoth*, innocent and unaware that it had died in his father's hands. Daniel planted a kiss on Gilla's forehead. Finally she moved and he was reassured that she was alive. She opened her eyes and extended her open arms to him.

⟫⟪

LATE Sunday morning, on his way to Gilla's house, Daniel saw Anita and Hershel descending the steps of the main church on Principal Street. Daniel was surprised by the sight and hid behind trees to avoid embarrassing them. He could not understand what might have motivated such an act. They were not religious Jews, but to attend church services was unheard of, even among the most atheistic survivors.

An hour later, Gilla's father drove into Sainte-Agathe in a white Cadillac Eldorado convertible. He had come to celebrate Gilla's twentieth birthday. Bright sunlight shone on Gilla's happy face as a photographer went around taking colored pictures of family and guests. Gilla posed with Daniel in the back garden. He was tall and dapper in a grey suit which had belonged to Evelyn's husband.

"They look like a Hollywood couple," the photographer remarked.

Gilla's father called for the music to stop. Standing at a high point of the lawn, with the bushes and lake road behind him, he thanked everyone for participating in this joyous occasion and then announced that the Cadillac convertible he had driven to Sainte-Agathe was Gilla's birthday present. Thunderous applause burst forth from the guests. Everyone was in high spirits. Daniel kept his eyes on Gilla and was happy to see that she was not overly excited by the gift.

⊰⊱

GILLA drove slowly up the road in the middle of the night to the hospital in her new car and parked it beneath the portico. She tip-toed to Daniel's room and roused him from his sleep.

"It's a beautiful night. Too hot to sleep," she whispered.

"How did you come here in the darkness?" he asked, afraid she might have walked.

"I drove. Let's go out," she proposed.

Sheila was awakened by the noise of their movements. "Where are you going?" she asked. She did not see Gilla who was waiting in the dim corridor.

"I'll come back soon," he murmured as he passed her bed.

"Can I come with you?"

"You need to sleep," he replied evasively.

Gilla skipped ahead of Daniel onto the front grounds. They stepped over the stone parapet around the pond. Gilla dipped her hand into the water. It was still warm from the long sunny day. She took her clothes off in the darkness and flung them onto the grass, then jumped into the pool. She was immodest, he thought, but could not deny that he was amused by her antics.

"Come, Daniel. No one can see us."

He doffed his pajamas and followed her in.

"Freezing!" he yelped quietly.

Gilla laughed and drew him close to her to warm his body with hers.

GILLA loved the summer rain and to run naked under the thick forest canopy where it never rained. As she ran, the sun freckles on her shoulders bounced up and down in a dervish dance. Daniel trailed behind her, listening to the voices of the creeks and the rustling of leaves in the wind. Having grown accustomed to the bush, Daniel no longer feared the unknown lurking behind the tree line.

One evening deep in the forest, they sat on a boulder mantled with patches of moss, facing a waterfall. The skies were brushed with the orange and yellow of a waning hot summer day. They had been berry picking. Gilla was feeding Daniel raspberries and he in turn was feeding her blueberries. A scene came poignantly back to him: his father stealthily exchanging plates with him in a camp where children were given tiny rations.

Daniel collected himself, then said: "I was thinking about a story my grandfather had once told me."

"Please tell me," she requested.

"It was a story about a poor farmer whose prize cow had died. Grandfather explained that the farmer had been decreed to die, but a saintly Jew intervened on his behalf and pleaded with God that the cow be taken instead of the farmer. And so it was that the cow died. There the story ended. To a child it made perfect sense, but to this day I regret not having asked my grandfather why the farmer had been decreed to die."

"Did you ever wonder about God?" Gilla queried. "When I asked my grandmother why we can't see God, she wrapped her hand in a kerchief and asked me, 'What is moving?' 'Your kerchief,' I answered at once. 'But what is making the kerchief move?' 'Your hand,' I replied. 'But do you see my hand?' she wanted to know, smiling, in anticipation of my answer that I didn't."

"Does that help you understand God?" Daniel asked.

"It did then."

"After the war I met a young woman in the Hamburg DP camp. Her name was Sophie. She was a survivor like me. I was eighteen and she was twenty-five. As we walked through the destroyed city, she told me what she had witnessed in the Kovno Ghetto. In October 1941, the Jewish Committee of the Ghetto was informed by the Gestapo that five hundred men were needed for 'intellectual' work in the main library. They were to be delivered by the Jewish Committee to the gates of the large ghetto the next day. But instead of the library, the Jews were taken to Fort IV of the fortifications surrounding Kovno. There the order was given to shoot them at close range in rows of a hundred at the edge of prepared mass graves. Sophie had witnessed it all," Daniel explained. "After that she forgot how to mourn. She admired Joseph Trumpeldor, the one-armed Zionist hero of Tel Hai. Sophie was determined to make her way to Palestine and wanted me to go with her to build a life together on a *kibbutz*."

"Do you regret not having gone with her?"

"No. We were friends, but we were not able to communicate with each other, imprisoned as we were in our own stories. We were both tied up inside bags.

Neither one of us could help the other… But you, Gilla, are outside everything I have lived through, so you can unfasten the knots on my bag."

"I really wish I could, so you would be happy and laugh."

"I want to laugh," Daniel murmured, but he knew he couldn't. He wished he could explain it to her. There were two possible lives he could lead. One life begins in a *shtetl* before the war and leaps over the war years with all memories of the war erased. He's a child with his mother, at her side, as they stroll together on a muddy street, in a world of synagogues and religious ceremonies, a world orbiting around the Torah. Then, suddenly he is in Canada, having leapt over the war years, to land safely in her arms with an absurd ambition to be a doctor. He is here enjoying precious days with her the willing receptacle of his memories. In this deleted trajectory of his life he does not share his war experiences with anyone for he has none. He is free of all war-time memories. His present does not include the painful past. But there is a cost: He must be an actor, living with partial memory, divided in two. The other choice is to live the life he is living now, weighed down by the memories that make him incapable of normal relationships.

"It's so sad. I always thought that more than anything, my husband would make me happy," she said reflectively, "that we would run in the forests, hand in hand, and never stop laughing."

"I learned in the camps that all pleasure is futile. After the war I tried to convince myself that it was not so, but then I say to myself, 'Daniel, be honest with yourself, how long does the memory of a kiss last? An hour? A day? Then what?' Then I am dead, if not by a German bullet, then by an accident, or else by your inevitable rejection." Daniel stopped for a moment, then added, "My fear of losing you prevents me from loving you."

"Why can't we just love each other without thinking about the past?" she put forward with child-like simplicity, an imploring smile shaping symmetric vertical crescents around the corners of her mouth.

"I cannot make anyone laugh," he answered. "I cannot make anyone happy."

Gilla's heart pounded with disappointment, but she refused to believe his gloomy prognosis. "Then I will make you happy! I promise! I can do it!"

She stood up and guided Daniel through bush to a canyon of towering pine. Along a mountain ridge nearby, the shadow of a cloud slithered slowly ahead of them and far below, a river emerged from the valley like the long tail of an animal. Wedged between a sunken tree crown and a partly submerged boulder, a broken red canoe lay on its side. All at once, the piercing cry of a crow was heard from the direction of Sainte-Agathe, the town which had become a sanctuary for Daniel. For the first time since his childhood, he felt sufficiently secure to try to peer into the future. He wondered if he would marry Gilla and raise a family in this foreign land, in a village named after a French saint, and not in the *shtetl* of his childhood. 'Dear ancestors,' he thought, 'look at what has become of your grandson!'

DR. MARQUIS called Daniel to his office in the middle of July and informed him that the most recent x-ray showed that all signs of his TB were gone. He was free to leave the hospital. The following morning Daniel packed his possessions into two shopping bags. He shook hands with the nurses and took leave of them. Daniel was relieved that Pinchus and George were not in the room. Meanwhile, Sheila was lying in bed. He moved toward her, but she thought he was walking out of the room and called to him: "You're walking out of here a healthy man. But me? They'll take me out of here in a box and you'll be watching the procession and you'll say, 'I should have danced with her.' Mark my words, you'll see."

Daniel had witnessed the deterioration of her health in recent months. As she clenched her mouth tightly, he perceived the bitterness of her failed life.

"Would you like to dance with me now?" he proposed, proffering his hand and a smile. "I'm ready if you are."

"No, no. Go, just go," she said gruffly.

Daniel could hear her sobbing as he turned to go.

"Wait!" she called to him. "Kiss me."

He bent over her and planted a kiss on her balding head.

George was waiting in the corridor, dressed in street clothes, as though he was about to accompany Daniel to freedom. He crooked his arm around Daniel's elbow and walked with him into the portico. A band of morning fog hung suspended over the mountain facing the hospital.

George continued the conversation they had left off a few days ago. Regarding his miraculous salvation from the mines by the atomic bomb, he needed to know whether Divine providence had worked through laws of probability: Was he the one in a million who always survives or was it the Hand of God that had reached out for him and hid him in the safety of a coal mine?

They saw Dr. Marquis approaching with his dog at his side as they were leaving the hospital grounds.

The doctor was carrying a sack of sweet corn for the nurses and patients. The dog ran up to sniff George's legs with its dank, black felt snout. George stopped and stiffened up until the dog ran off. Daniel nodded a greeting to the doctor as he passed. Having seen young women coming and going to and from the hospital in the middle of the night, it was apparent that the doctor was performing abortions, probably for valid medical reasons. Nonetheless, it conjured up the image of naked infant corpses he had once seen piled up against a wall.

Daniel and George took leave of each other with a friendly embrace. After one last look at the hospital and the front grounds, Daniel turned onto the country road and headed toward the village. Evelyn had agreed to let him stay in her basement while he prepared for his matriculation examinations. He had received a set of books from the Montreal Protestant School Board and was eager to get started.

⋯

THE SYNAGOGUE building was completed in late July. On the official opening day, two Torah scrolls were carried into the synagogue followed by a parade of dignitaries, including the mayor of Sainte-Agathe and a host of city councilors. The hotel owners and many of their guests gathered to witness the historic event. Notably absent were the card players. The internationally famous Cantor Shlomo Dressner from Philadelphia conducted the opening services, while the rabbi looked on. His wife sat demurely nearby, eyes lowered modestly, hoping no one would notice her.

The rabbi said a few words: "This new synagogue will help pull this generation of Jews out of the chaos of our recent history and deny Hitler his dream. The war has been over for several years, but now will come the complacency of uneventful times. It is these times that are dangerous for Jews. We must pray and learn the Torah daily and hope that these quiet years will not lead to another war and another slaughter of Jews."

When the ceremony was over, Anita and Evelyn danced the *hora* and invited everyone to join them. Gilla was there with her mother and sister. She glanced at Daniel and met his eyes. Then she and her sister entered the widening circle that had taken over the entire street. Soon she was dancing in the middle of the circle, her pleated skirt rising as she twirled on the precipice of abandonment.

Though Anita lost her faith in God due to the war, she could not contain her joy. "This day is ecstatic!" she cried out, testing a new word in her vocabulary. "I am so ecstatic!" she shouted, gesturing with exaggerated animation.

The ceremony was concluded with *Hatikvah*, the national anthem of Israel. With the synagogue now established, Evelyn Ramer officially assumed the post of President of the Women's Auxiliary which she had held *de facto* for many years. Enthusiastically, she made plans for rummage and cake sales.

"I know you saw Hershel and me coming out of the church," Anita said to Daniel later that day. "In Quebec you need the signature of a priest to qualify for adoption. We pretended to be Polish Catholics. There was no other way."

"You don't have to explain," Daniel said.

"I want to. There are one year-old twins up for adoption in the Gaspé. Their parents drowned in a fishing accident. They injected my breasts with something at Auschwitz and I stopped menstruating." She paused, then said: "Hershel and I are not religious anymore, but we're not Catholics either."

⌘

JULY was coming to an end and Daniel was preparing for the matriculation examinations scheduled for the coming week in Montreal. As he needed a rest from the books, Gilla suggested they spend the weekend at

Mont-Tremblant. Her father had driven the Cadillac convertible to New York City so they took her brother's motorcycle. Daniel sat behind Gilla as they sped north through the countryside on the Harley-Davidson, his arms wrapped tightly around her waist.

In a DP camp after the war, Daniel had heard rumours that his mother had survived and had gone back to their village searching for her relatives. Daniel had driven through a devastated Europe on a borrowed motorcycle, peddling packs of American cigarettes on the way. He searched the dangerous villages near Krakow for his mother in vain.

A heavy morning rain had quenched the thirsty fields, filling the hard furrows dissecting the fields of withering corn. Late morning, the rain had stopped and the sun was shining again. Elliptical shadows of fat, isolated clouds glided over the yellow fields. Holding the handle bars with one hand, Gilla pointed with the other to a message painted on a boulder on the shoulder of the road: *June 15, 1939 – Aaron Cohen and Brigitte Leblanc – forever.* She turned her head slightly to Daniel and said: "I wish I had known them."

They stopped at a gift shop where the sign, 'Christians Welcome!' greeted them. Moving on they came to a motel with an empty neglected outdoor swimming pool that separated the dilapidated, one-storey building from the highway.

"Are you Jews?" the young clerk asked.

"Yes," Gilla answered without hesitation.

"It is the policy of the owner to rent only to Christians. You would not want to stay here anyhow. There are crosses on the walls in every room."

Daniel noticed the attendant felt badly about what he was compelled to do. They mounted the motorcycle and took a side road to a small deserted lake. Along the rocky shore they found twigs and lit a fire. A swirling cloud of black flies trailed them as they settled under a tree and gazed at the sunset beyond the far end of the pristine lake. From the twilight forest, there wafted the gentle clamor of birds preparing for the night. Gazing at Gilla in the lambent light of the bonfire, he saw that something was troubling her.

"What's bothering my little girl?" he asked affectionately.

"The summer will be over in a few weeks, the hotels will close and Sainte-Agathe will be empty again. My father wants Heather to live with my aunt in Montreal so she can study in a Jewish school. And you'll leave me to study at the university. I'll be left alone with my mother."

"I'll come to visit often," he promised.

"You'll be too busy studying," she countered sadly.

"Then you'll come visit Heather and me."

"I suppose," she replied.

"Even if you came to live with me, what would you do all day?"

"I would cook and keep you company at night. Maybe I could find a job as a secretary?"

"You're not a city girl. You'll be bored and unhappy after a few days."

She shrugged her shoulders feebly, unconvinced. "All I know is that I want to be with you. I can't think of living without you. I love you. I remember my grandmother saying when I was a child, that she loves me like fire and water. I never understood what that meant, but I know that a fire burns inside me for you and I love you with all the moistness of my being."

He smiled, afraid to believe she could be devoted to him and at the same time live the free life to which she was accustomed.

"Would you really be happy being tied down to me?"

"I would be very happy. It's my dream."

"We have to get to know each other better."

"I feel I know you very well," she stated. "Don't you feel you know me?"

He nodded, but his heart held him back from a convincing 'yes'. "A few nights ago I dreamt we were the last survivors in the world and we decided not to have children so that civilization and all of history would end with us."

"That's a strange dream," she said, crinkling her brow.

"That would be my revenge."

"Against whom?"

He did not answer.

"Why do you want revenge?" she asked.

He was happy she did not understand. "It was just a dream," he consoled her. "I really want to have many children and to name them after my parents and my sisters, and everyone else I lost."

"What about my grandmother?" Gilla asked wistfully. "She passed away two years ago. Couldn't we use her name also?"

He was taken aback by the assumption she had inferred, although he could not deny that he had lured her into it.

Daniel and Gilla did not sleep that night. Early in the morning a large fish crashed through the glassy silence of the lake.

THE FRAGRANCE of lilacs filled the streets of Sainte-Agathe as Daniel walked to Gilla's home with a fast and happy gait. Twilight was settling over the village. Above the western horizon, the moon lit up a gap between clouds in the shape of a hand. He had spent the long hot day studying and was looking forward to the planned jog with Gilla around the lake. The clear purple sky was sprinkled densely with stars. Gilla was standing in the distance in front of her family garden, the turbid, mote-filled light of sunset entangled in her hair. As he approached her, she noticed that one of his shoelaces was undone. When finally, they were standing next to each other, she bent down on one knee and tied his lace for him, while Daniel played piano on the spheres of her exposed spine. As his hand lingered on the smooth cataract of her hair, he reflected on his good fortune and, for a moment, forgot his unrelenting fear that he would certainly forfeit it all. Gilla stood up, dampened her forefinger on her tongue, then rotated it in the air until she located a propitious direction. With a flourish of her arm, she beckoned him to follow her. Trotting slowly at first, she wagged her ankles and wrists, limbering up. Daniel trailed lamely behind, coughing to justify his sluggish pace. The forests around them smelled lusciously earthy, and along the lake, the reflection of pine trees followed them like an endless train. Gilla stopped from time to time, waiting patiently for Daniel to catch up to her. As he approached her, he exaggerated a grimace of exhaustion to which Gilla responded with a burst of laughter. She gave Daniel an admonitory slap on the back and off they went again. He feigned a fast move, but they both knew he was not yet healthy enough to take the lead.

"Not too fast," she cautioned. She meandered from one side of the road to the other, to allow Daniel to keep up with her. Now and again they linked hands, cantering along as one, the lake gurgling quietly below escarpments. Her stable pace allowed his eyes to wander across the purple frescoes of the sky. He would dart ahead occasionally on longer stretches and look back, imbibing the amorphous dance of her untethered breasts. Distracted, he nearly ran headlong into a tree.

"Be careful!" she shouted, then burst into laughter.

Then in a valley mist, he suddenly lost sight of her, the black hiatus of night wedged between them. It was the moment he had always feared. He called to her through the darkness, but there was no answer.

"Gilla! Gilla, where are you?" he shouted in desperation as the terror of her absence possessed him.

Just as he was convinced he had lost her forever, he caught a glimpse of her wincing face as she fought through a gust of wind.

"Where were you?" he called in disbelief and joy.

"Just a few feet ahead of you."

Their fingers strained to touch in the darkness and when they did, his last trace of doubt was dispelled. He was happy, suddenly remembering or permitting himself to remember what it must be like to live without fear, to feel secure. In this release, he became playful, childlike. He began chasing her, flinging burs at her back. She took up his joyful spirit in kind and would feign disapproval, brandishing a forefinger in reproof, pirouetting in front of him before she set off for another chase. When at last they returned to Gilla's home, Daniel had returned to his usual self and was feeling foolish, guilty even, about his outbreak of joy. Noticing the change in him, Gilla put her hands on his shoulders and turned him toward her.

"Daniel, you'll see," she vowed. "When we'll be ninety years old, we'll also jog around the lake. That'll be so much fun."

-⁂-

THE TOP of Gilla's convertible was down and the wind lifted her hair as she and Daniel headed to Montreal early on a sunny morning in mid-August for Daniel's matriculation examinations. From the crest of a hill just north of St. Jerome, Daniel looked across the shimmering plain of farm land to the city spread around a mountain shaped like a sperm whale.

Gilla gave him a kiss for good luck and dropped him off at the High School of Montreal on University Street. She planned to spend the day at her aunt's house and then meet Daniel at the Roddick Gates of the McGill University lower campus at eight o'clock in the evening.

The examinations were much easier than Daniel had expected. He had prepared for much more difficult questions. Left with lots of extra time, he checked his answers repeatedly. Afterwards, he went to the Roddick Gates to wait for Gilla, eager to share with her his confidence that he had done well. When she failed to appear by nine o'clock, he grew worried. He found a pay phone and called Gilla's aunt. The woman explained that Gilla had learned that a Serbian folk dance group was performing at Beaver Lake on Mount Royal. She had decided to go there and meet Daniel afterward.

Concerned, Daniel took a taxi to Beaver Lake.

He could hear the loud music coming from the park behind a row of trees as he stepped out of the car. Searching the parking lot for Gilla's car, Daniel found it with the top off. He made his way through the darkness to a large crowd of young people standing around the performance area. After circling the area twice, he found

Gilla sitting drunkenly on a bench, a bottle of beer at her side, vomit on her dress. He kneeled down beside her and tried to look into her drooping eyes.

"Gilla!" he called, until he had her attention. She feigned a smile with lips parted, reeking of liquor. Her head flopped from side to side, drool hanging from her mouth. Mumbling apologies, she tried to explain what had happened. Daniel carried tissues in his back pocket. He wiped her face as best he could, then helped her stand up. Lifting her into his arms, he carried her to her car.

"I'm so sorry," she mumbled as he lay her down on the back seat.

He doffed his wind breaker and placed it on her. Fortunately, Gilla had forgotten the key in the steering column. Daniel drove pensively through the darkness as she slept all the way to Sainte-Agathe. He had known Gilla for eight months. An undeniable bond existed between them and an understanding that they would get married in the future. However, Daniel could not suppress an uneasiness about her reckless carousing. Whether he could succeed in curtailing her excesses and bring her into a stable lifestyle was the foremost question on his mind. Gilla was a warm and kind young woman who genuinely cared for him, but was this enough on which to build a lifelong relationship?

SATURDAY night an Israeli dance troop that had been touring the U.S. was scheduled to perform at the Sainte-Agathe public beach. The shore was lit up by bonfires. It had rained in the afternoon and now the wet wood smoked, crackling in the night air, reflecting shimmering patches of light far out into the lake. The guests headed down to the beach where the spirited young Israeli dancers were huddled, ready to start.

The dancers' lean bodies were intertwined, leaping over each other in a dazzling performance. These young representatives of the State of Israel infused life into the downtrodden survivors, who were exuberantly thankful for every scrap of pride and joy. It was a magical, redemptive moment for the survivors: The Jewish nation was still alive and their suffering had not been entirely in vain.

After the performance, the dancers mingled with the guests on the beach as waiters served slices of watermelon, chocolate muffins and tea. One of the dancers was a handsome young Israeli with curly red hair. Gilla must have caught his eye. In the midst of the laughter and chatter, Daniel saw the dancer approach Gilla with hand extended in greeting. They exchanged words while Daniel watched from a distance. Then distracted for a moment by Evelyn who wanted to know how the matriculation examination went, Daniel lost sight of them. Alone again, Daniel began searching the crowd for Gilla with anxiety mounting every second. He finally caught a glimpse of her and the dancer walking up the path toward the hotel, in what seemed a furtive escape from the beach. He tried to discern where they were heading but kept losing sight of them in the darkness behind trees along the lake road. A cold sweat covered him as he immediately assumed the worst scenario. How could this be happening? Daniel felt as though his life was being torn from him. Once again, he was fifteen, on the death march, his dying father in his arms.

Gilla returned to the beach after what seemed a very long time. She was searching for Daniel, distraught and dishevelled.

"Daniel! Daniel!" she called to him, but he pretended not to hear and walked away in the opposite direction before she could see him. He imagined she had become so habituated to acts of deception, that her tryst in the forest meant little to her. Daniel had learned in the camps not to detest fraud or treachery—they were merely human characteristics, like being tall or thin; but betrayal was another matter entirely. Now nothing could stanch the spurting blood of the mortal wound Gilla had inflicted on him. He knew that the passage of time would not dull the pain. His life was shattered, no less than when he had entered Auschwitz for the first time. Daniel hated himself for having been lured away from the life of loneliness he had resigned himself to before meeting Gilla. Her cheerfulness that had drawn him to her was an ingenious guise for an incurable promiscuity. Now her manifestly immoral behavior had made her utterly repugnant to him.

DANIEL saw Gilla on the road near the hotels the next day. He walked right past her as if she was not there. She was confused and burst into tears. In the ensuing days, Gilla struggled to understand the sudden icy detachment in Daniel's bearing. She sent letters to him via Sandra, but Daniel would not read them. Gilla lingered outside Evelyn's house waiting to meet him. When he emerged from the basement door, she greeted him, but he responded with indifferent nods.

"Did I do something wrong?" she pleaded in despair, a pathetic pitch in her voice, and grabbed the sleeve of his shirt. "Please tell me! Please. I love you!"

"If you truly loved me you would know what pains me!" he said harshly and broke away from her grasp. His anger was palpable and she collapsed in sobs.

"Daniel, I don't know you! Who are you?" she wept.

So certain was he of what had occurred that fateful night, that there was no need for him to confront Gilla. He remained inconsolable, his face drawn with sadness and disillusionment.

※

THE NEWS that Daniel had been admitted to the Bachelor of Science Program at McGill University came to Evelyn in a telephone call on the last day of August. On the second day of September, she accompanied him to the train station where he would take the nine o'clock morning train to Montreal. Evelyn was troubled by the conflict between him and Gilla.

"Is there anything I can do?" she asked solicitously. "You're such a wonderful couple. Everyone was hoping you would get married. It would be so beautiful."

"Do you remember when you picked me up here ten months ago?" he replied, shifting the topic of conversation.

Evelyn nodded respectfully, sensing that Daniel preferred to remain silent.

※

DANIEL'S first day in Montreal was devoted to exploring his new neighbourhood. He walked north from his basement room in the ghetto to the very end of Fletcher's Field and the boundary of the neighborhood nurturing Europe's survivors. A soft autumn rain was falling and the sidewalks were black, spotted with white flecks of chewing gum. He imagined the ghetto cordoned off by French speaking SS officers, hauling Jews from their houses, shoving them toward Fletcher's Field for transport to a camp with a French name.

He walked along Duluth Street on his way to McGill University, past the stone walls of the Hotel-Dieu Hospital, then a playground, and through the tunnel under Park Avenue that reeked of urine. Emerging on the far side, he was greeted by the steep mountain slope of Mount Royal with its cross on top. He proceeded to Pine Avenue and from there to University Avenue. The Royal Victoria Hospital and the Montreal Neurological Institute stood high on the mountain to his right. He turned left and entered the campus from its high point along University Avenue. After a long day of walking, he returned to his basement room.

Daniel lived on Clark Street near Bagg Avenue where children played street hockey on roller skates. The ornate Beth Shlomo Synagogue was at the corner of Bagg and Clark. One block south and on the opposite side of Clark Street stood the Beth Yitzchak Synagogue, with its wooden steps painted grey. Its shed like appearance resembled the synagogues Daniel had frequented with his father before the war. He felt at ease among the old men, but could not pray. Saturdays at dusk, Daniel sat in a corner on a splintered bench, listening to the familiar Sabbath songs and watching the men munch *shmaltz* herring and drink Kik Cola.

He found part-time work in stores along the Main, the central avenue of the Montreal Jewish ghetto. Evenings, Daniel worked as a cashier at the Warsaw Fruit Market. For Oberman Brothers Kosher Butchers, he was a delivery boy, and on Saturdays, he packed phonographs for twenty cents an hour. Later in September, Daniel found employment in a fish store. Handling the spiky, slimy fins of dories without gloves caused an infection in his right arm. The large vein from his thumb to his shoulder was painfully inflamed. A kind, Gentile coworker accompanied him to the emergency room of the Hotel-Dieu Hospital nearby on St. Urbain Street, where he received injections for a week.

Although Daniel met many people, mostly older survivors, he kept to himself and concentrated on his studies. Gilla often came to his mind. He was no longer angry, but felt disappointed in himself for having become involved with such a woman.

After a few weeks into his courses, Daniel was able to follow lecturers clearly and to comprehend the textbooks. One Friday night, he met a young Jewish girl in the library. Freda was a short, spirited woman he became acquainted with in spite of her communist views. He wanted to forget Gilla and when Freda invited him to a Friday night bonfire on the mountain, he accepted. Jewish students danced and sang songs of the pioneers who had settled in Palestine. While sitting on the grass near the bonfire, he recalled a bonfire in the *shtetl* square celebrating the holiday of *Lag Ba'Omer*. Now he was an adult in Canada, sitting among students dreaming of bonfires in Israel.

⚜

THE HIGH Holidays came at the end of September. Daniel accepted an invitation from Evelyn and returned north for the celebrations. The train moved swiftly past fields of harvested corn standing with bowed yellow heads. Daniel saw the rabbi's wife on his way from the train station, wandering the streets in her long black dress, looking at the clouded autumn sky.

The sound of the ram's horn coming from the direction of the synagogue reminded him of the *shofar* call of his childhood, when fear and trepidation for the Days of Awe gripped man and child in the streets and alleyways of the bustling *shtetl*.

Only one hotel remained open, catering to wealthy guests who had come up for the holidays from Montreal. The other hotels were shuttered for the winter. Daniel stayed in Evelyn's basement.

"Were you planning to visit Gilla?" Evelyn enquired once Daniel had finished eating supper on the evening of his arrival.

"No," he replied. "I came to visit you and my friends at the hospital."

⊰⊱

A SOFT autumn rain pebbled the surface of the lake as Daniel and Evelyn walked along the road to the synagogue on the evening of the first night of *Rosh Hashana*. There were a few women present and barely a quorum of ten men. The rabbi's New Year sermon analyzed a verse in the third chapter of Ethics of the Fathers: 'When man is called to account,' which the rabbi connected to *Rosh Hashana,* the Day of Judgment. Daniel countered in a whisper to himself: "When God is called to account."

Daniel noticed that neither Gilla nor her mother

had come to the synagogue for morning services. Heather was present, sitting next to Anita and her newly-adopted twin sons, who were asleep in a double carriage. Daniel approached Heather after the services and asked her if she knew where Gilla was.

"In the woods."

"Where in the woods?" Daniel asked.

Heather shook her shoulders. She did not know.

Daniel followed a familiar path deep into the forest to the 'horsey tree' as Gilla had called it. As soon as he passed through a copse to the clearing where the tree stood, he saw Gilla. She sat with her back to him, slouched forward in a fetal position. On hearing footsteps, she turned lethargically, looked up, then gave a trembling start on seeing him. A sudden burst of sunlight revealed the pain on her wincing face. She greeted him with a fearful grin. Her cheeks were sunken, lips desiccated, eyes glazed with tears. Her uncovered arms hung at her sides as if holding heavy suitcases.

"I came to walk you home," he said.

"You don't love me anymore," she muttered in a low, staccato voice. "What have I done?"

"We've changed," he stated evasively. She strained to rise from the 'horsey tree'. He could not bring himself to help her up.

"You don't speak to me anymore," she drawled

quietly, afraid to look up at him.

They walked slowly through the forest in sullen silence. She was shorter and thinner than he remembered. At length, he felt he had to say something.

"Your favours are extended to everyone. I didn't feel I was special to you. You give yourself to whomever shows the slightest interest in you and the worst of it is you don't see anything wrong in spreading your generosity around." He had prepared these words, hinting at the cause for his detachment, yet careful not to openly accuse her.

"I don't know what you're saying. I love you, only you."

Gilla lowered her eyes, her face dimmed, then said regretfully, desperately searching for an explanation that might appease him: "My scarred breast makes me feel like a cripple. Maybe that's why I'm friends with everybody."

"I'm also crippled, but I don't go about cavorting with everyone I see," he declared, keeping his eyes averted.

She toddled slowly at his side. "Tell me what you think I did and give me a chance to explain. Please give me a chance."

"There's no need for an explanation," he said obstinately, knowing in his heart there was none.

-»€«-

DANIEL returned to Montreal to continue preparing for midterm examinations. A week later, while in Montreal visiting her brother, Sandra stopped in on Daniel to deliver a letter from Gilla. Daniel took the letter, thanked her, then put it aside. Despite his resolve to ignore it, he opened the envelope and read the letter an hour later.

> *My dear precious Daniel,*
>
> *I love you. Why don't you believe me? I no longer go to the train station to dance. I only volunteer at the hospital to help patients and I study Judaism with Sarah, the rabbi's wife. My mother was not converted properly so I plan to convert myself. I thought this may be the reason you rejected me. Sarah told me about it, how I'll have to immerse in the lake at the end. I can't wait to get there. I hope with all my heart that this will make a difference in your feelings for me. I know sometimes people are given a second chance. I beg you for a second chance. If not, I have nothing to live for.*

A photograph of them together on a boat was in the envelope. On the back Gilla wrote: "I love you forever." Although the letter touched him, he could not assuage the feeling of having been deceived. The fidelity he had naively expected in the relationship had existed only in his mind. He was certain there could be no other logical conclusion to her behaviour that night. He felt justified in assuming the worst and was prepared to live with the consequences.

━━◆━━

DANIEL walked to the port where, almost a year ago, a woman from the Jewish Immigrant Aid Service had greeted a thousand new arrivals from Europe. In broken Yiddish, she had promised the vacant-eyed survivors that food and shelter awaited them. They slept on blankets on the YMHA gymnasium floor that first night. Then in the morning Daniel ventured into the streets. The black, ankle-high running shoes he had been given were tight, but he no longer felt pain in the toes that had frozen on the last death march. His pants were held up by a blue cord that served as a belt. As he walked through Fletcher's Field, he was surprised to hear people speaking French. The park was partitioned by a wide thoroughfare where cars and horse drawn wagons moved beside rattling electric trams. Beyond a grassy field, the mountain rose sharply to a large cross that loomed over downtown.

They were given English lessons in a small windowless room in the basement of the YMHA, where Daniel sat suppressing a growing cough. The teacher assured the students that the grammar they were learning now was much easier than the Hebrew they had studied before the war. The last time Daniel sat in a classroom was in the spring of 1939, when he was nine years old.

He was finally assigned a room on Esplanade Street facing Fletcher's Field, which he would share with two other young camp survivors. Above them, an alcoholic doctor performed tonsil operations late into the night. The screams of children drew Daniel into dim tunnels of forbidden memories. One morning, Daniel met the doctor in the vestibule and broke out coughing. The doctor noticed the blood on Daniel's lips and teeth and sent him for a chest x-ray at the Royal Victoria Hospital. The diagnosis came back: tuberculosis. A few days later, Daniel was on his way to the Mount Sinai Hospital north of the city.

⸺⸱⸺

DANIEL received a letter in late November from Evelyn, marked 'URGENT' on the envelope.

Dear Daniel,
  Gilla's father died of a heart attack in a restaurant

in Manhattan. Please call Gilla. At least write to her.

That night Daniel responded:

To Miss Gilla Steinberg,

    I am very sorry to hear about your father. I will try to come and see you as soon as I finish my examinations. Then I will try to explain. It's time I got everything off my chest.

    Best wishes, Daniel.

The loneliness in the city was diminishing the intensity of his disappointment in Gilla. One night, after a long day of lectures and study, he wrote another letter, its tone neither angry nor forgiving, merely expressing a desire to communicate with her. Gilla's next letter arrived soon after. Daniel inferred a tone of excitement in its lines. Since the letter was not stamped, he inferred that it must have been hand delivered by Gilla herself.

My dear, precious Daniel,

    It took almost a week for your letter to arrive. I saw the post office date stamp. A week is such a high mountain to climb. One can hardly see anything over it. Your letter caught me by surprise. I had been extremely depressed all day. My mother is so ill. I hide everything from Heather in Montreal. Anyhow, after a lonely walk around the lake, it hardly seemed possible that a letter of yours would be waiting for me. I trudged up to the mailbox on the lake road, put my fingers inside the mailbox and felt something. I removed my hand, my thoughts being far away with you, and began to descend the slope to the house. Halfway down, it suddenly occurred to me that there was a letter in the mailbox. I leaped back up the snowy slope, scuffled with my keys, finally unglued the tiny silver one from my fingers, and opened the box. And I wasn't disappointed; there you were for me to press to my lips and crush in my hands. How neatly and uniformly you write; it looked as though the letter had been typed. It's hard to imagine that a year ago you could hardly write a word of English. And how formal you are: MISS GILLA STEINBERG, all in capital letters. Why the MISS? I smiled for the first time in many weeks when I saw that. I'm not a MISS. I'm just plain Gilla. I stood there on the road clutching your letter as cars passed me. Wonderful memories swarmed over me as I carried the precious prize to my room. That was an hour ago. It's after midnight now and I'm sitting at my desk with the fisherman lamp lighting up your letter. It came at such a crucial moment. How terribly forlorn I've been feeling since I last saw you! But as soon as I saw your letter, this awful mood was broken. Your

*letter saved me, no less than a hand reaching out to
a drowning man or should I say, woman? I thank
your kind heart for feeling my grief. How sweet and
wise you are, my precious prince. Reading your letter,
I recall the wonderful times we had together. Do you
remember the walk around that little square lake in
Mont-Tremblant? It was beautiful, wasn't it? When
will I see you? I anxiously await your answer. And
please, please, do not feel that you have to explain
anything to me. Love with all my heart.*

Yours forever, no matter what you decide. Gilla.

—⟫⟪—

ANOTHER letter arrived from Evelyn in December.

Dear Daniel,

*I feel bad disturbing your studies and to bring you
not such good news. Gilla has not heard from you for
two weeks and is convinced you have decided to leave
her forever. That, her father's death, and her mother's
illness have made her very depressed. You know
how she used to walk around the lake. One day she
walked off the road and right onto it. Her footprints
were found in the freshly fallen snow on the public
beach and her frozen body on the ice in the middle of*

the lake. Fortunately, the water had already frozen strongly and she did not break through the ice. An old fisherman found her, lifted her onto his sled, and brought her to the shore where she was resuscitated. It was truly a miracle. God had mercy on her. To this day, her mother does not know what happened. Gilla is recuperating in the hospital under the care of Dr. Marquis. I do whatever I can for Gilla's mother. I visit her every day and prepare meals. Someone has to do it. I don't know if you'll want to come back here now, but I had to tell you the truth. One more piece of bad news. The rabbi and his wife are getting divorced. Sarah is now living with me. It's very sad.

Evelyn Ramer.

Daniel felt he would not be able to go on if something were to happen to Gilla. He thought that if, in the camps, he had been promised a safe haven on condition he marry an unfaithful woman, he would have certainly seized the opportunity. Now he had a safe haven and an unfaithful woman.

Daniel took the train to Sainte-Agathe. It had snowed recently, and the red fire-hydrants along the streets of the town were dressed up with white snow caps like miniature Santa Clauses. On the way to Gilla's house, he encountered a large black dog on a leash, sniffing adamantly for old scents deep in the snow around a hydrant. Electricity poles, a procession of high crosses, accompanied Daniel across town. On the streets, lumps of dirty gray snow lay strewn about like dead rats.

Having forgotten his gloves, Daniel's fingers were near-frozen. He descended the slippery hill sideways to the front door. There was no response to his knocking. The door was unlocked. Doffing his boots in the vestibule, Daniel stepped silently across the dim living room to the staircase leading to the basement. A standing lamp lit a spherical hole in the large room. Gilla was sitting on the sofa, her legs drawn up on the couch. On seeing him, her mouth gaped open, a tenuous but joyous expression on her face. He stood rubbing his frozen fingers.

"Come here," she beckoned, lifting her skirt, inviting him to place his frozen hands between her warm thighs. As he leaned down to her, she covered his blue lips with her open mouth, breathing warmth into him. He kissed her with loving forgiveness, then with passion. There was a blue filament vein on her forehead. He kissed it and thanked her for taking him back. She did not ask for an explanation. Enraptured by her soft and supple body, the old accusations were irrelevant. Gilla wept uncontrollably. For a long time no words were exchanged. She caressed his face, touching and not touching the contours of his cheeks and chin. When she thought he was about to say something, she whispered: "You don't have to. It doesn't matter. We're together—that's all that matters. Please love me. Never leave me again."

"Never, never," he promised with heavy, sniffling sobs, happy that she bore no resentment.

⚜

DANIEL paid the hospital a quick visit before returning to Montreal. He learned that George had died of pneumonia in St. Jerome. Sheila had been admitted to a psychiatry ward in Montreal, and Dr. Marquis's wife had passed away a week earlier. The funeral at the main church in Sainte-Agathe had been impressive, Daniel overhead the nurses say. The polished cherry wood casket had cost five hundred dollars. "What a pity to bury such a casket!" one of the nurses had remarked.

⚜

THE DECISION to return to Gilla brought Daniel peace of mind. Thrusting doubts and suspicions aside, he concentrated on his studies. He talked with Gilla on the phone every day and took the train every Friday afternoon to Sainte-Agathe. The walks in the countryside and the silence of the winter forests were a welcome change from the noise of the city. Meanwhile the health of Gilla's mother was deteriorating. Dr. Marquis had prescribed a new medication which calmed her nerves, but made her sleep most of the day. Gilla spent long hours with Sarah learning the laws of Judaism over the winter months. Sarah was happy for Gilla's formal conversion and for her planned wedding in the spring, as she wept for her own childless and failed marriage.

⊰⊱

DANIEL began borrowing Gilla's motorcycle and driving it to and from the city once the roads were free of snow and ice in the early spring. This saved him an hour each way. The Laurentian Mountains were still marked by the remnants of ski trails the first time he took the motorcycle out. Along open stretches of highway, Daniel inhaled the fresh cold air. Then approaching Sainte-Agathe on his return, he opened the throttle fully. Gilla was waiting for him on the outskirts of the town, anxiously anticipating the familiar echo of the motor from beyond the huge boulders defining the final bend in the road. Then, at last, her longing was relieved by the roar of an engine. Sound turned into image as a young man, head uncovered, holding one handlebar, waved to her with the other arm. She ran to him before he could get off the motorcycle and they kissed passionately.

"You're so late. I was afraid something had happened to you!" she cried tearfully, then mounted the seat behind him. She embraced him tightly as they drove along the lake road to her home, past the synagogue where the rabbi sat alone on the front veranda, studying.

⁓⁓⁓

IT WAS the night of Gilla's scheduled immersion in the lake to complete the process of conversion. Daniel had accompanied her to the synagogue where the rabbi sat engrossed in his Talmudic studies. The rabbi had forgotten to shake off the ashes of the cigarette he was holding in his upraised hand. A wilting tower was about to crumble onto the open pages of the tome. As he turned around to greet his visitors, the ashes fell and he immediately blew them off the pages.

The rabbi stood up, donned his black bowler hat, and accompanied Gilla to a quiet stream that fed the lake. There, behind a tree, Gilla disrobed, and stepped solemnly into the cold water. From a distance the rabbi saw her completely immersed. He called to her to come out. Gilla ran to the shore, trembling and dried herself with a towel. Later, she tried to describe the feeling of transcendence she had experienced while immersed in the lake. Daniel listened to her excited words, smiling indifferently.

❧

GILLA and Daniel accompanied Sarah to the train station for her trip to Montreal. She was wearing her long black dress and holding a single valise. She had become very thin since her arrival the previous spring. The following morning she would meet her husband at the Rabbinical Court where the marriage would be formally ended.

"We'll miss you," Gilla said, holding her in her embrace.

"I'll miss you as well," Sarah murmured sadly in her British accent and with a wan smile. "Perhaps one day you will visit me in England."

On the way back from the train station, Gilla turned to Daniel and said: "Sarah once told me that God Himself makes marriages. How could He make such a mistake?"

"Perhaps Sarah's mission in life had been to come to the north to befriend you and to teach you. And who knows who you will teach in the future?"

Daniel realized that his words sounded like his grandfather's, but it did not trouble him and seemed to satisfy Gilla.

-)(-

THE WEDDING took place on a hot Sunday afternoon in June. Respecting Jewish tradition, Daniel and Gilla fasted. Daniel had a headache, causing him to narrow his eyelids against the bright sunlight. The night before the wedding Gilla had immersed herself in a stream on the outskirts of Sainte-Agathe, this time accompanied by Evelyn.

Evelyn had made alterations to a wedding dress she had borrowed from a friend in Montreal and gave it to Gilla. Two horse drawn wagons, painted yellow and brown with rubber wheels, brought the couple separately to the synagogue. Family and friends gathered on a grassy field overlooking the lake. A photographer was busily taking family pictures on Albert Street with the lake for background. Anita pressed her twin boys to her cheeks and tried to smile, but smirked awkwardly instead. One of the twins began screaming for no apparent reason. Hershel tried to comfort him, but referred to him by his brother's name, so this had no effect on the child.

The rabbi spoke briefly about the fragility of life.

"Why is there so much rejoicing at a wedding? The Zohar explains that the two souls of the couple were one before they were sent down into this world in two separate bodies. At the wedding the two souls are reunited."

Then with the heel of his shoe, Daniel broke a wine glass wrapped in a cloth napkin, and Daniel and Gilla became man and wife.

A group of twenty boys from a Yiddish school were bussed in to liven up the wedding by performing Cossack dances. Guests faced each other in two lines, and ran towards each other, meeting in the middle, then ran backwards to their original places, only to repeat it all over again. Gilla danced joyously with the women. She jumped onto a table, unrestrained in her gestures. Daniel danced with the men, reserved, possessed by memories.

A reporter from the Canadian Jewish Weekly came from Montreal to attend the first Jewish wedding in Sainte-Agathe. A week later his review would appear: *The marriage of Gilla Steinberg, daughter of Mrs. Ginette Steinberg and the late Mr. Sonny Steinberg, to Mr. Daniel Edelman, son of the late Mr. and Mrs. Edelman, was solemnized in the newly built Beth Shalom Synagogue on the shores of Sainte-Agathe on Sunday, June 16, at five o'clock, by Rabbi Chaim Bender. The bride was given in marriage by her mother. She wore a white gown, trimmed with lace and laced-pearl-beads; fashioned with a boat-shaped neckline; long sleeves; the A-line skirt, with a long train. Her veil was attached to a beaded tiara; and she carried a prayer book with white orchids and lilies-of-the-valley. Miss Sandra Ramer of Sainte-Agathe was maid of honour. Her pink gown was appliquéd with lace and had its own jacket. She had a flowered headdress and carried a bouquet of pink roses. Mrs. Steinberg, mother of the bride, wore a sleeveless pink brocade gown and a bluish pink hat. Isaac Levy of Halifax was best man. An eight-piece orchestra played to two hundred and fifty guests. The groom has no living relatives.*

III

❧❦

MASADA

❧❦

A TIGHTNESS was forming in Daniel's chest as he found the August 20th, 1952 entry in Gilla's diary. With trepidation, he began reading.

"One of the Israeli dancers asked me to show him directions to Lakeside Inn where the troop is staying. He didn't understand my instructions so I went with him to the main road, then to the fork. His English was terrible and I didn't speak Hebrew. I pointed to the left to follow the path to the hotel. As I turned to go back to the beach to find Daniel, he took my hand and pulled me to him and tried to kiss me. I pushed him away and began screaming. When I was free of him I ran back to the beach. I searched for Daniel but couldn't find him. I'm so afraid of something."

Daniel lowered the diary to the table and stared blankly into the Jerusalem traffic, his heart beating rapidly. If what Gilla wrote in her diary was true—and why should she lie to her own diary?—then his life these past sixty years had been based on a complete fallacy. He looked down again at the diary. Subsequent pages were covered with scribbling: 'Daniel's coldness is torture.' Unintelligible words were scribbled here and there. He deciphered: 'He hates me!' scrawled in large capital letters. Daniel stood up and started back to the hotel, an old broken man plodding along slowly in the scorching midday heat of Jerusalem. He left Gilla's briefcase at the reception counter for safekeeping.

━▶❦◀━

DANIEL registered for the Masada tour and was given a paper bag containing a sun hat, two water bottles, and a guide map. He did not go to his room, nor did he leave a message for his son. As he stepped out of the air-conditioned lobby into the parking lot behind the hotel, a wall of heat struck him. The tourists began boarding the bus at 1 pm. Minutes later, they were pulling out of the hotel. Exhaling slowly, Daniel watched the landscape turn from green to yellow. Then the bus veered right onto Highway 1 where cultivated terraces of olive groves corrugated the yellow mountain slopes. Olive trees with their arthritic branches gave way to shrubs, then to sand, as the bus headed into the Judean Desert.

The Israeli guide stood on the entrance step of the bus next to the driver, facing the tourists. Speaking in a heavily accented English, he pointed out battle fields from the War of Independence. The charred and rusted remains of military vehicles and tanks, turrets still proudly upright on hilltops, substantiated the history lesson.

Daniel sat with fists clenched, possessed by his thoughts of that fateful night in the north, oblivious to the guide and the chatter of the tourists around him. He was tormented by the shameful secret he had kept hidden. The dark accusation which he had never expressed in words had impaired every part of his life. That silent and cruel indictment, based on an entirely false premise, had destroyed Gilla's life. Daniel could not ward off the demons that now made his life unliveable. But on the battlefield in his brain, the written facts could not entirely overcome the conviction of sixty years. At the center of this certainty was his resistance to believe in Gilla's love. The war had calloused his ability to have faith in good. No logic could defy this feeling.

The bus came to a military checkpoint. Israeli soldiers informed the driver of a kidnapping in the Hebron Hills, then waved the bus on. The guide kept reading from a script: "Masada is located at the top of an isolated rock on the edge of the Judean Desert and the Dead Sea Valley, between Sodom and Ein Gedi. The top of the rock is flat, elongated from north to south. Four hundred and forty meters high, Masada is isolated from its surroundings by deep gorges on all sides."

On hearing the height of Masada, a desultory

thought that had been ricocheting in his mind, suddenly gained clarity. Daniel converted the height of Masada to a measurement of time: the four hundred and forty metres were the eighty-four years of his life. Each meter equalled a fifth of one year. By climbing the mountain, Daniel would relive his life, and along the way, he would correct the many errors he had made.

The guide continued: "The location of Masada forms a natural fortification and fortress. It was the last bastion of Jewish freedom fighters against the Romans. It is a site of both tragedy and heroism. It is a site of a mass suicide, where the remaining Jewish rebels took their own lives by leaping from the cliffs."

Through the front bus window, Daniel glimpsed the imposing white mass of Masada in the distance. When the bus reached the parking area, the guide cautioned the hikers to cover their heads and explained that there were two ways to ascend: by hiking up the snake path or by taking the cable car. He recommended that anyone not in good health take the cable car.

The sun bore down on the tourists as they stood in the open among the buses gathered there. Daniel wiped the sweat streaking from his brow. Next to him was a group of mostly elderly German tourists who had just arrived from Tel-Aviv. Daniel flinched at the grating sound of their sibilants uttered with unrepentant arrogance. "The venomous prattle of incurable predators," he thought. With his back partially to the sun, Daniel's forefinger which he had raised to his eyes, projected a short stubby shadow on the upper lip of a cleanly shaven man standing nearby. Even the sun was conspiring against him.

The guide repeated his warning to wear hats and to drink plenty of water. Daniel inhaled with slow, shallow breaths. As the tourists began the ascent, a sudden gust of wind blew Daniel's cap off his head. Minutes later, he slipped on a rock. A young woman came to his aid, offering an outstretched hand and Daniel regained his footing. He looked up to thank her and she smiled, a smile that reminded him of his oldest sister.

The guide strode up and down along the line of weary but cheerful climbers, reminding everyone to keep hydrated. About half-way up the mountain, the slowly advancing column suddenly came to a stop. A woman was screaming in German. The guide came running down the trail, shouting: "Someone collapsed! Does anyone know CPR?"

"I'm a doctor," Daniel announced.

"Come quickly!" the guide called to him.

Daniel lurched clumsily after the guide, following him over stone steps along rising slopes. A bald elderly man lay flat on his back. Wide suspenders arched up and over the massive dome of his stomach, holding up

Bavarian shorts. He wasn't breathing. Daniel bent down, felt for a pulse but couldn't find any sign of life. He asked the guide if there was a defibrillator on the bus. There wasn't. Daniel checked the stricken man's airways while his wife fell to her knees crying hysterically. Daniel glimpsed at her through the sweat pouring into his eyes. With one hand on top of the other, Daniel administered fifteen hard compressions on the man's chest, then gave him two breaths and checked the airway again. He delivered another fifteen compressions and gave him another two breaths. There was still no sign of life. At the thought that the man might die in his hands, he shuddered. "Breathe, you cursed Nazi!" he snarled. The tourists saw the numbers tattooed on his forearm and were silent. Daniel and the guide sat the lifeless body up, head lolling down and around. On hands and knees, Daniel went behind the man and performed the Heimlich maneuver. Suddenly rattling was heard from the man's chest, then there was a cough followed by another and the man began to breathe on his own. The man's wife was beside herself with joy. The guide and two men pulled the victim into the shade of a rock outcropping.

"A medical helicopter is on the way," the guide assured everyone. A stretcher was brought up from another bus.

No longer needed, Daniel scuffled through the crowd that had gathered around him. Someone extended a bottle of water to him. He took it and drank.

Meanwhile the tourists were told to return to the base to await instructions. The guide informed them that the military police had closed the road to Jerusalem because of the kidnapping and that they would be spending the night at a Dead Sea Hotel. The tour would resume early the next morning for those who wished. There would be another bus for those who chose to return to Jerusalem in the morning.

⟫⟪

BULLET holes pocked the white stone facade of the hotel. Inside, a pleasant young Arab woman greeted the weary tourists with a smile. Exhausted from the heat, Daniel went to his room and fell into bed. Lying restlessly next to a noisy window air conditioner, he remembered that it had been more than two days since he had taken his medication. As his chin drooped to his chest, he noticed a large black splotch at the bottom of the left breast pocket where his ball point pen was leaking blue blood from an old bullet hole in the heart. He had another shirt in the Jerusalem hotel room, but none with him here.

After searching for his father in the hotel in Jerusalem, Benjamin discovered at the reception that he had gone on the Masada tour and that the tour group had been forced to spend the night at a Dead Sea Hotel. Worried for his father's health, he called a cab, but was told that the road blocks made access to the Dead Sea impossible. Accepting the advice of the clerk, Benjamin hired a motorcyclist who knew how to circumvent blockades. Benjamin finally arrived at the hotel in darkness under a starlit desert sky, surprising his father who was pacing along the beach, head bent, his hands clasped behind his back. Hotel guests were still frolicking in the sea.

As father and son walked side by side, Daniel recounted the incident with the German that afternoon.

"You did what you were trained to do," Benjamin said approvingly.

Daniel was silent. He felt a sudden urgency to clarify Gilla's memory in his son's mind. But at the same time he could not bring himself to tell him what he had read in Gilla's diary.

"All these years I didn't trust your mother," he confessed. "I want you to know that I was wrong. I'm responsible for her death. I killed her as much as if I had stabbed her with a knife." A clod of lead in his heart had fallen from him.

Benjamin girded his mental loins, relying on the Talmudic skills that had guided him through difficult situations in the past with his father.

"Mom had prepared me. She knew you would tell me this one day," he responded thoughtfully. "She knew your suspicions although you had never stated them to her. I was her confidante. She was always faithful to you and loved you, although you questioned that love."

It was painful for Daniel to hear those words.

"Go back to Jerusalem," he instructed his son. "I'll come in a day or two. First, I must climb Masada."

"I'm not leaving without you," Benjamin declared at once in calm defiance of his father's command.

⁂

BENJAMIN slept in Daniel's room on a cot that was brought in, while Daniel spent the night sitting agitatedly in the hotel lobby. At dawn, through a window, a corner of another window became visible, full of sparkling light from the rising sun. Benjamin came down to the lobby, holding a prayer shawl and phylacteries he had borrowed from a guest before retiring for the night. He had left his own in the Jerusalem hotel, planning to return before morning. While his father was drinking coffee, Benjamin recited the morning prayers in a corner.

Daniel observed. He had never donned a prayer shawl or phylacteries in his life. He wondered for a moment how it must feel, but the sudden clatter of a chair falling in the breakfast area startled him from his wayward thought.

Before leaving the lobby, Daniel stopped at the reception desk and handed the Palestinian woman behind the counter a hundred U.S. dollar bill.

"No! No!" she insisted, blushing, refusing to take it.

"For your children," he insisted.

"I have no children," she replied, smiling modestly.

"You will," he answered and left the money on the counter. It was important to him that at least one person in this world think well of him.

The tourists began trickling groggily out of the hotel in the incandescent light of an Israeli morning. Father and son made their way across the dusty road to the gathering area at the foot of the mountain. Benjamin took hold of his father's forearm from time to time, but the old doctor wanted to show him that he could walk on his own. A sidelong glance at his son stirred memories of Daniel's father on the final death march. Benjamin was now the same age as his father was then and to Daniel's surprise, he recognized resemblances in his father's features. Glancing up at the mountain that awaited him, Daniel hoped to accomplish on the slopes and cliffs what he had failed to do at his wife's grave.

Accompanied by a noisy bustle, the motley troop of tourists set off on the ascent of Masada. Daniel thrust himself forward, followed by Benjamin. As they climbed, Daniel made forays into the village of his childhood, which stood suspended in the eerie silence of memory. All around him a red haze clung to the mountain coping, cradling the *shtetl* like the thick crayon sketch of a child.

When a woman threw off her sandals and took to walking barefoot, it was Gilla Daniel saw walking barefoot along the deserted Sainte-Agathe beach on an autumn day, the stem of a withered rose wedged into her hair, the once winsome face of a happy young woman gone. Then behind Daniel in the queue winding up the face of Masada, a child was crying, evoking the memory of a little boy in shorts he had once seen in a camp yard, lying face down, suckling a stone on the footpath.

The higher they climbed, the less Daniel was aware of the extreme heat and the noise of the tourists around him. His consciousness was leaving him. He was reliving the interview for admission to the McGill Medical School. He still spoke English with a heavy accent and worried if this would harm the interview. "What qualifies you over hundreds of other applicants?" a doctor had asked him. Daniel had not wanted to state that his grades were nearly perfect as this could be regarded as boasting. He realized the interviewers were questioning the essence of his character. He raised the sleeve of his jacket and with lowered eyes, displayed the numbers on his forearm and immediately regretted doing it.

Now, less than an hour into the ascent of Masada, Daniel felt faint. He slipped under the iron balustrade and rolled down the hillside, coming to rest against shrubs sticking obliquely out of the sand. His son ran after him, stumbling and falling down the rocky slope until he reached his father. Fallen, lying twisted, eyes closed, Daniel was remembering a bright summer day much like this one in the north. Gilla was standing on a step, the sun behind her shining into his eyes. He could only see her dark, shadowed face and parts of her silhouette as she turned left then right.

Now it was Gilla kneeling before him as Benjamin lifted his head into the crook of his arm and gave him water to sip.

Benjamin felt his father's pulse and looked into his bloodshot eyes. The old man's face was scraped but did not seem otherwise injured. Taking a handkerchief out of this pocket, Benjamin soaked it with water from his bottle, then washed his father's face. High above them along the trail, the tourists had come to a stop and were looking down at the fallen old man.

Daniel was determined to climb back up and rejoin the others. Benjamin wanted him to rest, but the old doctor crawled stubbornly over the scorching sand and rocks. With the help of a young German woman who had followed him down the slope, Benjamin was able to stand his father up.

An hour later, to everyone's surprise, Daniel was the first to reach the summit of Masada. He stood with head lowered and inhaled slowly as sweat poured from his face. The tourists streamed past him but he did not see them. Benjamin stood nearby, also bent over, perspiring and out of breath. Daniel reached out and grasped his son's hand and pulled him close. Through blurry eyes he saw the wife of his youth standing before him and burst into tears. Embracing his son, mouth wide open, Daniel kissed him awkwardly on his wet, shiny forehead, whimpering with contrition. The old man had forgotten how to kiss. Benjamin, too, was weeping.

"Do you remember when we went into the forest to cut down dead trees?" Daniel asked between gasps. "It was in the late seventies. Your mother was still alive."

"Yes." It had happened no more than two or three times when Benjamin was a teenager. "Mom was afraid we'd get hurt with the chain saws or a tree would fall on us. But we had a good time and we'll do it again,"

Benjamin promised.

"Yes, for sure," the old man averred, as if giving his word to an official agreement.

As they moved into the shadow of a refreshment tent nearby, Benjamin reminded his father: "We have a flight to catch."

Daniel nodded: "Yes, my son, we have a flight to catch."

Far below them, the Dead Sea, a blue ribbon against the backdrop of the jaundiced Jordanian hills, reminded Daniel of the rivers and emerald valleys of the north.

-End-

ABOUT THE AUTHOR

ABRAHAM BOYARSKY is the author of several novels including "Schreiber" (1982, General Publishing) for which he was awarded the *Canadian League of Poets' Gerald Lambert Memorial Award*; "The Number Hall" (1992, Oberon Press) winner of the *Toronto Jewish Literary Prize*, 1994; "A Gift of Rags" (1995, Lester Publishing); "The Ratcatcher" (2007, Oberon Press); "The Chassidic Trauma Unit" (2016, 8th House Publishing); a number of short stories including the collection, "A Pyramid of Time" (2015, Amazon LLC); and the mathematical textbook, "Laws of Chaos" (1997, Birkhäuser Basel) with Prof. Pawel Gora. He currently lives in Montreal where he is a full professor of Mathematics at Concordia University.

Other books by this author

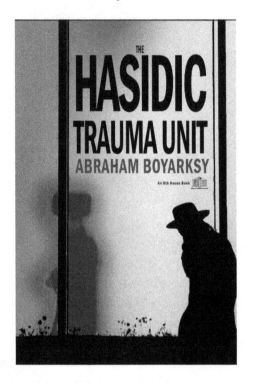

THE CHASSIDIC TRAUMA UNIT by Abraham Boyarsky
5. 5 x 8 | 228 pages | ISBN 978-1-926716-40-4 (pbk.) | $19.95

Sender Pleskin is a self-proclaimed trauma specialist dedicated to serving his Chassidic community and to 'gently' nudging it into modernity. When a Bubmer Hasid child falls inexplicably into a coma, Sender and his team jump to action. Hunting down leads in his investigation, Sender follows the signs that he interprets to be Divine Providence as they lead them down a circuitous path that will test not only his faith, but all he was and is.

"Through this fast-paced novel, replete with kidnappings, espionage and fugitive war criminals, Abraham Boyarsky captures the Chassidic communities, their lives and their voices."